## Elizabeth Ferrars and The Murder Room

>>> This title is part of The Murder Room, our series dedicated to making available out-of-print or hard-to-find titles by classic crime writers.

Crime fiction has always held up a mirror to society. The Victorians were fascinated by sensational murder and the emerging science of detection; now we are obsessed with the forensic detail of violent death. And no other genre has so captivated and enthralled readers.

Vast troves of classic crime writing have for a long time been unavailable to all but the most dedicated frequenters of second-hand bookshops. The advent of digital publishing means that we are now able to bring you the backlists of a huge range of titles by classic and contemporary crime writers, some of which have been out of print for decades.

From the genteel amateur private eyes of the Golden Age and the femmes fatales of pulp fiction, to the morally ambiguous hard-boiled detectives of mid twentieth-century America and their descendants who walk our twenty-first century streets, The Murder Room has it all. >>>

## The Murder Room
### Where Criminal Minds Meet

**themurderroom.com**

T0352525

## Elizabeth Ferrars (1907–1995)

One of the most distinguished crime writers of her generation, Elizabeth Ferrars was born Morna Doris MacTaggart in Rangoon and came to Britain at the age of six. She was a pupil at Bedales school between 1918 and 1924, studied journalism at London University and published her first crime novel, *Give a Corpse a Bad Name*, in 1940, the year that she met her second husband, academic Robert Brown. Highly praised by critics, her brand of intelligent, gripping mysteries was also beloved by readers. She wrote over seventy novels and was also published (as E. X. Ferrars) in the States, where she was equally popular. *Ellery Queen Mystery Magazine* described her as 'the writer who may be the closest of all to Christie in style, plotting and general milieu', and the *Washington Post* called her 'a consummate professional in clever plotting, characterization and atmosphere'. She was a founding member of the Crime Writers Association, who, in the early 1980s, gave her a lifetime achievement award.

*By Elizabeth Ferrars*
(published in The Murder Room)

*Toby Dyke*
Murder of a Suicide (1941)
  aka *Death in Botanist's Bay*

*Police Chief Raposo*
Skeleton Staff (1969)
Witness Before the Fact (1979)

*Superintendent Ditteridge*
A Stranger and Afraid (1971)
Breath of Suspicion (1972)
Alive and Dead (1974)

*Virginia Freer*
Last Will and Testament (1978)
Frog in the Throat (1980)
I Met Murder (1985)
Beware of the Dog (1992)

*Andrew Basnett*
The Crime and the Crystal (1985)
The Other Devil's Name (1986)
A Murder Too Many (1988)
A Hobby of Murder (1994)
A Choice of Evils (1995)

*Other novels*
The Clock That Wouldn't
  Stop (1952)

Murder in Time (1953)
The Lying Voices (1954)
Enough to Kill a Horse (1955)
Murder Moves In (1956)
  aka *Kill or Cure*
We Haven't Seen Her Lately
  (1956)
  aka *Always Say Die*
Furnished for Murder (1957)
Unreasonable Doubt (1958)
  aka *Count the Cost*
Fear the Light (1960)
Sleeping Dogs (1960)
The Doubly Dead (1963)
A Legal Fiction (1964)
  aka *The Decayed Gentlewoman*
Ninth Life (1965)
No Peace for the Wicked (1966)
The Swaying Pillars (1968)
Hanged Man's House (1974)
The Cup and the Lip (1975)
Experiment with Death (1981)
Skeleton in Search of a
  Cupboard (1982)
Seeing is Believing (1994)
A Thief in the Night (1995)

# No Peace for the Wicked

## Elizabeth Ferrars

An Orion book

Copyright © Peter MacTaggart 1965

The right of Elizabeth Ferrars to be identified as the author of this work has
been asserted in accordance with the Copyright, Designs and Patents Act 1988.

This edition published by
The Orion Publishing Group Ltd
Orion House
5 Upper St Martin's Lane
London WC2H 9EA

An Hachette UK company
A CIP catalogue record for this book is available from the British Library

ISBN 978 1 4719 0718 0

www.orionbooks.co.uk

# CHAPTER ONE

When the small gray-haired woman in the brightly flowered silk suit appeared in the doorway of the hairdresser and hesitated there in the warm sunshine, as if she were making up her mind whether or not to take a taxi, the man who had sat for the last hour in the coffee bar on the other side of the street got up and strolled out on to the pavement.

Lighting a cigarette, he stood looking up and down the street. Cupped around the flame of the match, his hands hid most of his face except for the watchful black eyes. But his shabby brown suit with narrow trousers, his dusty down-at-heel shoes, his smooth black hair growing low in a peak on his forehead had by now become unpleasantly familiar to the woman.

"There he is again," Antonia Winfield said to herself. "It's the same man—I'm sure it is—or am I going mad?"

Walking slowly, she turned in the direction of Piccadilly.

Every little while she paused to look at antiques in a shop window, or at lace tablecloths and colored bath

1

towels. When she did this, the man on the other side of the street paused to inspect expensive foreign shoes or embroidered blouses.

The bewildered disquiet in Antonia's blue eyes increased. It was such an extraordinary feeling, this being furtively, distantly followed. Too extraordinary, too senseless to be actually frightening, yet quite unnatural, as if a dream had dragged on from the nighttime into the day.

"But I'll know for sure in a moment," she thought. "If he follows me into Farr's, or if he's waiting for me when I come out, I'll know I'm not imagining things."

She stood still to gaze into a window full of handbags.

In a mirror at the back of the window the reflection of the man in brown stood still to look at a display of gloves and stockings.

Suddenly Antonia found it difficult not to hurry, not to try to escape from him at all costs. She resisted the impulse, and when she came to the entrance of Farr Tours Limited she strolled straight past it, as if she had no thought of going in. It was only when she saw that the man, on his side of the street, was well past the entrance too that she turned, walked quickly back and went through the revolving doors into the booking hall.

Weaving her way through the crowd inside, she went toward the clerk who always made the arrangements for her holidays abroad and who had promised to have her tickets ready for her that day.

He was busy with another customer, but he saw her, smiled and said, "Good afternoon, Mrs. Winfield. I'll be with you in just a minute."

His friendly recognition did her good immediately. Her world, which had been teetering off balance, grew steady. Smiling back at him, she sat down at the counter to wait, inconspicuously easing her feet out of her high-heeled shoes. Almost casually she glanced over her shoulder.

The man in the brown suit was standing just behind her.

A wave of cold swept through her.

Yet what did it matter if this madman had taken it into his head to follow her? There was nothing that he could do to her. Not here, at any rate. Not if she managed to shake him off before she started for home. The home in which, as it happened, she would be quite alone for the next two nights, since Roger had started that morning for Scotland.

But she never minded being left alone in the house, and had always been irritated by the sort of woman who made a fuss about it. Yet just then she found the thought of her empty and silent home on the edge of the Heath decidedly less attractive than usual.

Apparently the man was paying no attention to her. He had picked up a leaflet from the counter and was reading it. She saw that the hands that held the leaflet had long supple fingers with black-edged nails. His face was sharp-featured with a muddy skin, a tight, nervous mouth and thin, black eyebrows.

Turning away from him, looking fixedly at a poster on the wall of a Spaniard fighting a bull, Antonia tried to think. Should she or should she not appeal to the clerk for help? Should she say to him that, unlikely as it seemed, this person standing just behind her had been following her around all day and that she couldn't bear it any longer, so would he please call a policeman?

The person would naturally deny it. He would say that he hadn't even been aware of her existence till that moment, that obviously she was just another of those peculiar middle-aged women. The poor clerk would be deeply embarrassed and when next she came in he would look at her with dread and would hurry away, leaving her to some stranger who knew nothing about her or what she wanted.

Folding her hands together in her lap, she set her teeth and waited.

"Now, Mrs. Winfield." The clerk turned to her as the customer ahead of her departed. "I've got everything ready for you, if you'd just like to check it."

He opened a folder full of papers and spread them on the counter.

Antonia took as long as she could to go through them. She looked most carefully at tickets and traveler's checks, at reservations for her seat on the train to Dover, for her sleeper on the train to Venice, for her cabin on the ship to Athens. She read what was written even in small print on the vouchers for her accommodation in the hotel in Athens and the hotel on the island, an island which, so certain friends had told her, was one of the only spots left in Europe where the quiet as well as the sunshine could be guaranteed.

Antonia hoped that what they had told her was true, for it looked as if she was going to need the quiet very badly by the time she got there.

While she looked at the papers and signed the traveler's checks, she chatted brightly to the clerk, delaying as long as she possibly could the moment when she must leave him and start back across the booking hall with the un-solved problem of the man in brown at her heels. But the moment couldn't be put off forever. At last she found the resolution to say, "Thank you so much, Mr. Borrow, I'm sure you've thought of everything."

Putting the papers back into the folder and the folder into her handbag, she turned toward the door.

Behind her the man in brown gave a sharp sigh, as if patience had at last been rewarded. Moving quickly into the place that she had left, he put his elbows on the counter and started talking to Mr. Borrow. When Antonia looked back from the doorway she saw the two of them with their heads together over a timetable.

The anticlimax was almost as unnerving as her fears had been. For clearly the man had not been following her at all. It had been sheer hysteria to think so. Obviously, he had merely been doing the same things as she had herself, coming in from Hampstead on the same bus, shopping in the same shops, having lunch in the same restaurant and then ending up at Farr's, because, like her, he was going abroad for a holiday.

At least, it seemed no more unlikely than that he should have been following her.

Yet as she went on, Antonia could not help glancing back several times and it was only when she reached Madame Julie's, where she was to pick up a dress that she had bought the week before and that had had to be altered for her, that she really began to believe that the man in brown had dropped out of her life.

This visit to Madame Julie's was Antonia's last errand of the day and she was thankful that it was, for her feet were hurting and she was very tired. No doubt that was largely the result of her ridiculous fears. Strange fears for her to have been distracted by all of a sudden, not her own sort of fears at all. Like most people she could suffer short agonies of anxiety for insufficient reasons, feeling convinced that she had been unintentionally rude to someone who would never forgive her, or that there was dry rot in the roof which it would cost thousands of pounds to put right, or that she was just experiencing the first symptoms of a mortal illness. But she had never before taken it into her head that she was being pursued up and down London streets, into shops, into restaurants, by sinister men who looked as if they slept in their clothes and didn't wash much.

She frowned, remembering the restaurant. That was the most difficult thing to fit in. The man had come in a minute or two after she and her friend Enid Wells had settled themselves at their table. He had sat down at a table near the door and, never once glancing at them, had read a newspaper while he ate. Then he had gone out before them, but not until they had started signaling to their waiter that they wanted to pay their bill. And when they had emerged into the street he had been standing on the other side of it, lighting a cigarette, just as he had been later on, when Antonia had emerged from her hairdresser's.

However, he was gone now and it was time to start forgetting him.

Going into Madame Julie's little shop, where Antonia had bought most of her clothes for the last few years because she had convinced herself that they were just a little different from those that you saw everywhere else at the same sort of price, she sank down wearily on to the gilt sofa near the door and reminded the young girl who came over to her that she was Mrs. Winfield and that she had come to try on the dress that had had to be lifted at the shoulders. The girl went to fetch Madame Julie, who appeared after a moment, bringing the dress.

She was a stout, friendly woman with impressively controlled hips, glossy black hair and an unidentifiable foreign accent, which Antonia suspected of having been cultivated in some London suburb.

"And this year you go again to Greece, no?" Madame Julie said as she helped Antonia into the dress. It was a straight white shift with a bold pattern of big blue and green flowers. "How I envy you. And of course you travel by train, as always? I too, when I can. It is the natural way to travel. We were never meant to fly in airplanes. When I am compelled to fly in the course of my business, I nearly die of fear. There . . ." She fastened a broad gilded leather belt with a handsome buckle around Antonia's waist, stood back and looked her up and down in the long mirror. "The dress is perfect now, madame. That little alteration on the shoulders makes all the difference. You can wear it with or without the belt, as you like, but for you, I think, is better with. More slimming. But it is a matter of taste."

"Oh yes, I like the belt," Antonia said.

She liked the dress too and herself in the dress. She always liked bright colors and bold patterns. Also she liked very much Madame Julie's happy knack of remembering so much about her customers. Like Mr. Borrow's recognition in Farr's, it helped to reduce the feeling it was so easy to have that in the middle of London you were in a kind of desert with no real people around you, that anything could happen to you there, that you could drop straight through a hole in the pavement and nobody would notice. Chatting about her coming trip abroad, Antonia's nerves simmered down to normal.

But as she presently sat back in the taxi that was taking her home, she thought, "I'll have to be careful, all the same, if this is what happens to me as soon as Roger goes away. It won't do if I think I'm being followed by strange men all over Europe. Or at least they'd better be tall and handsome, with motives I can understand."

She smiled, shut her eyes and relaxed, at last beginning to be amused by her experience.

The Winfields lived in a row of little Regency houses with rounded bow windows, elegant fanlights over the doors and small front gardens full of roses, irises, lavender and pinks, almost as if they were still in the country.

When the taxi stopped at her gate Antonia made sure that she had picked up all her parcels. Then she paid the driver, walked up the short path to the door and, as she let herself in, decided to make herself a cup of tea and take it out to the garden at the back of the house. Then presently she would have a bath, put on a dressing gown and sit with her feet up, reading the detective story that she had brought home from the library yesterday, and when she felt like it, she would boil an egg for her supper and go to bed. Carrying her parcels into the small white-paneled sitting room, she dropped them onto the Biedermeier sofa and started down the basement stairs to the kitchen.

She was halfway down when the front doorbell rang.

She considered ignoring it. She did not want to risk spoiling her program for a nice restful evening. But she realized that whoever was ringing had probably seen her taxi arrive and would know that she was deliberately hiding. Returning up the stairs, she went to the door and opened it.

A fair-haired girl in a crumpled cotton dress stood there. With one hand she was grasping a suitcase, with the other a sodden handkerchief into which she was fiercely blowing her nose. Above the handkerchief tear-reddened eyes gazed at Antonia.

"Why, Tessa!" Antonia exclaimed in distress. "My dear girl, whatever's happened?"

Tessa Foley pocketed the handkerchief and asked in an unsteady voice, "May I come in, please, Antonia?"

Antonia moved aside to let her in, then shut the door behind her.

"But what's wrong, Tessa?" she asked. "It isn't Alec, is it?"

8

"Of course it's Alec," said the girl.

"He's hurt? He's . . ." Antonia stopped herself. She could not remember ever having seen this niece of Roger's cry before. His favorite niece, incidentally, the one most like him. She was normally as calm, as even-tempered as he was himself, as unwilling to make any parade of her feelings. "It isn't—anything serious, is it?"

"Call it serious, or call it the funniest thing on earth, I don't mind," Tessa answered. She put the suitcase down and gave a long sigh. She was slim and tall and had Roger's aquiline face, finely arched eyebrows and deepset gray eyes. "It had to come, I've known that for some time, and I was perfectly all right until I was almost here and then for some reason I started to cry. I'm very sorry. But you needn't worry, I've stopped now."

"You're telling me you've had a quarrel with Alec, is that it?"

"I've left him," Tessa said.

"I see. Hm. Well." Antonia frowned, feeling stupid and useless. "Well, I was just going to make some tea. I think I'll go on and do it and you can have a wash and then we can talk."

"If you don't mind, I don't think I want to talk much," Tessa said. "There's really nothing to say. I just need somewhere to stay for a short time while I make a few plans. May I stay here for a few days, Antonia?"

"As long as you like, only Roger's away in Edinburgh and I'm leaving for Greece tomorrow. But if you don't mind being alone here, of course you can stay."

"Oh . . ." There was a quaver in the girl's voice. "I'd forgotten about your going away. Perhaps I'd better think of something else. It isn't that I mind being alone, but I'm not sure what I'd do if Alec came here, making scenes. He won't do that while you're here, but if he knew I was alone he might start anything."

"Well, you'd better stay tonight," Antonia said. "I'll go and get the tea now and we can have it in the garden."

But while she was making the tea she realized that for Tessa in her present state the garden would be rather public. Taking the tray up to the sitting room instead, Antonia waited there, hearing the girl moving about in the bedroom overhead, and wondering what Roger would do about the situation if he were here.

Tessa was a responsibility that he took very seriously. She was the only child of his youngest sister, who had depended on him a great deal after the death of her husband in the war. But two years ago she had suddenly married a Canadian and had gone to live in Toronto. She had expected Tessa to go with her. But Tessa, without consulting anyone, had abruptly left the drama school where she was supposed to be a fairly promising student, and had taken a job as a secretary in a firm of publishers of scientific books. There she had met Alec Foley and three months later had married him.

Roger had been very worried about it all at the time. He had said that Tessa had married only to get even with her mother and that that was a pretty bad reason for marrying. Besides, she had thrown away a talent and was bound to regret it. But then he had taken a liking to Alec and had said that perhaps he had been wrong and it would work out after all.

Now it wasn't working out, but Roger was in Scotland.

Walking aimlessly about the room, waiting for Tessa, Antonia fretted at her own dislike of responsibility. She hated having to make decisions that affected other people, people, that is, who were close to her. She found nothing easier than giving advice to people she knew nothing about. She could sort their problems out for them in no time. But when someone she cared for was in trouble, she only became anxious and muddled, and wanted Roger to tell her what to do for the best.

When Tessa reappeared she had changed out of her crumpled cotton dress into a loose white shirt and narrow black slacks. She had washed her face, put on fresh lipstick, brushed her hair and somehow forced herself into a rather formidable composure.

Taking a cup of tea from Antonia, she said, "I'm sorry about being a nuisance like this, but I promise I won't mess up your plans in any way. I think if I can have just a day or two to get my breath, I'll be able to see what I ought to do next." She sat down on the sofa. "What's Roger doing in Edinburgh?"

Responding to the girl's quiet tone, her careful matter-of-factness, Antonia answered, "He's doing some external examining in the University. Poor man, he's been complaining about having to do the job ever since he agreed to take it on, trying to make me think he hates it. Really, of course, he's delighted, because it gives him such a wonderful excuse to go a little further north for a fortnight's fishing and not come to Greece with me."

"I thought you'd given up trying to persuade him to go abroad with you long ago," Tessa said.

"Yes, I had," said Antonia. "I know he hates the heat almost as much as I long for it. But this year Enid Wells, who usually goes with me, had to cancel everything because her daughter's having her first baby and Enid wants to be with her. So Roger was afraid I might put some real pressure on him to come."

"Won't it be rather depressing, going alone?" Tessa asked.

"Oh, I don't think so. I'm always very good at being lazy by myself. But now about you, Tessa, and this breathing space you say you need—"

"Please!" Tessa's eyebrows twitched nervously. "I've left him. That's all there is to say at present. Let's go on talking about Greece. Where are you going this year?"

"Wait a minute," Antonia said. "I only want to talk about this breathing space because I've been wondering what you'd think—if you're sure, really quite sure, you know, that you need it—about coming away with me. At our expense. No—" She raised a hand and hurried on as Tessa tried to speak. "It's only an idea I've just had and I'm not sure it's a good one, but when you're thinking over what you want to do, keep it in mind. Then if you think it would help in any way, we can see what we can fix up tomorrow."

From the way that Tessa's eyes went suddenly wide and blank, there might have been something terrifying in this suggestion that straightaway she should go so far from her husband. For a moment she said nothing. Then she gave a curious little smile. She stood up, stooped over Antonia and kissed her.

"You're a darling," she said. "You're the only person I could face being with at all just now. But about going with you . . ."

"My feelings won't be in the least hurt if you don't want to," Antonia said. "In any case, I half expect by tomorrow you may think it's a better idea to go home. But think about it, just in case."

"I was only going to say, if I came with you, I'd be rather dreary company," Tessa answered, sitting down again.

"If you were too dreary, I'd pack you off sightseeing by yourself," Antonia said. "All I'm interested in myself is doing absolutely nothing at all. I've had a frantic year with all my committees and things. The last of its kind I mean to have, that I swear! When I've had a good rest and got

12

back a little strength of will, I mean to resign from the lot."

"I think I've heard you say that before," Tessa said. She went on thoughtfully, "But I could pay for myself. I've brought some money away with me. You know, I think it's the perfect solution. Alec won't be able to follow me and make scenes, and with luck he may begin to think about some of the things I've said and realize I mean them. And then perhaps we can talk. I don't know—perhaps not—but I know we'll never get anywhere until he starts to listen to me occasionally."

"Talking of being followed . . ."

Antonia stopped and Tessa looked at her questioningly.

"Oh, nothing," Antonia said with a self-conscious laugh. She got up and went to fetch the packet of cigarettes that lay on the table in the little bow window. "It's just that I did an incredibly stupid thing today. I managed to convince myself I was being followed all over London by a terrible, sinister-looking man. Can you imagine me thinking a thing like that? After all, I'm not actually unbalanced, am I? I saw him first at the bus stop—"

Her voice dried up in her throat. She started to shake.

He was out there on the pavement, staring straight in at her.

# CHAPTER TWO

Tessa looked up at her quickly, then came to her side.

By the time she reached the window all that was to be seen of the man was his back as he walked away down the street. He wasn't hurrying. He wasn't trying to avoid being seen. He was simply walking along. He looked just like any man going about his normal business.

In a moment he was out of sight.

Antonia's fingers felt numb as she opened the packet of cigarettes. In a high-pitched voice she said, "It's completely absurd, I know it is, you don't have to tell me."

"What's absurd?" Tessa asked.

"That wherever I go, I see that man."

"Which man? The one you were starting to tell me about, or the one out there?"

"Both—they're the same!" Antonia broke the head off the first match that she struck and had to light another. "I saw him first at the bus stop this morning, as I was telling you. I don't suppose I'd have looked at him twice if I hadn't thought he was Jack Singer, one of the tech-

14

nicians in Roger's department, and that I ought to talk to him. But he didn't seem to be taking any notice of me and I'm always awfully bad at people's faces, so I didn't say anything. But I looked at him again and when he turned his head a little, I saw that really there was only a superficial resemblance. So then I forgot about him and went on to do some shopping. I went to Simpson's and Fortnum's and one or two other shops, then I had lunch with Enid and then had my hair done. And wherever I went, there he was."

"He went and had his hair done at your hairdresser's?"

"Don't look at me like that, Tessa! No, of course not."

"What did you mean then about his being there?"

"He was waiting on the other side of the street when I came out. And he followed me to Farr's and while I was getting my tickets from Mr. Borrow he stood just behind me. And then . . ." In the telling of the story Antonia's voice had dropped to its normal pitch. Moving away from the window, she sat down again. "Then he didn't follow me out. He stayed behind and started talking to Mr. Borrow himself. So I thought the way we'd kept running into each other all day must have been coincidence. I convinced myself that if we both came from this neighborhood and both wanted to go to Farr's, it was quite natural for us to meet again and again around Piccadilly. Almost natural, anyway. More natural than that a man like that should have been following someone like me around all day."

"A man like what?" Tessa asked. "I didn't see him properly."

"Oh, an awfully ordinary, shabby sort of man, half my age."

"I thought you said he was sinister."

"I'm quite sure he's sinister. But it didn't strike me at

15

once. I don't think he *looks* sinister, except for his hands. I noticed them when he was standing behind me in Farr's. As a matter of fact, when I saw how long and clever they looked, I thought perhaps he was going to try to pick my pocket. I even wondered if he could somehow have known that I was going to pick up a fair sum of money in traveler's checks and had been following me around to steal them. But it was just when I'd got them that he dropped me."

"Perhaps when he saw the masterful grip you took on your handbag."

Antonia hit the arm of her chair with her fist. "Don't laugh at me, Tessa! Every word I've told you is true and it hasn't been at all funny!"

"I'm sorry, I'm not laughing, I'm just thinking," Tessa said. "I was wondering if you can really be sure it was the same man you saw here just now."

"Oh yes, it was the same man!"

"But this man in Farr's has been on your mind all day, and you said yourself you aren't good at faces, and if he's really so ordinary-looking—"

"It was the same man!" Antonia's voice shot up again. "I haven't gone out of my mind."

"But look at it reasonably—"

"Now wait! Just wait a moment, my child!" Antonia began to let herself go. She enjoyed the feeling of it. Her anger took the chill out of her veins. "Have I had the impertinence since you came here today to suggest you should look at your own troubles reasonably? It might in fact be an excellent thing for you to do, but I don't consider it my business to tell you so. I consider it something for you to do in your own way and your own time, and that's the spirit in which I expect you to listen to my troubles. It's the only one which is ever of the slightest use. That's something I've learnt on some of my committees—Marriage Guidance, Unmarried Mothers and what not. Other people's reasonableness is normally just an insult."

Tessa smiled. "All right, I'm sorry, it was the same man. But in that case it seems to me we ought to tell the police about him."

"And have them advise me to see my doctor, as you're on the edge of doing?"

"But I'm not," Tessa said. "I admit I still think it's possible the man you saw here was someone quite innocently admiring your garden and not the same as the other one, but if you're sure about him—"

"Oh, now I'm to be humored! I'm mad, but no one's going to mention it."

"I was just going to say," Tessa said patiently, "if you don't want to call the police, mightn't it be a good thing to telephone Roger?"

"And ask him if he's put a detective on my trail, to see how I behave when he goes away?"

"Darling, you're being rather difficult, aren't you?" Tessa crossed the room, knelt down on the hearthrug at her feet and put her elbows on Antonia's knees. "I just meant we could ask Roger to come home, as you're so worried," she said.

There was a short silence.

Then, with a smile, Antonia said, "There—I've calmed down. The crisis is over."

"But don't you think we ought to let Roger know about it?"

"And ruin his fortnight's fishing? I wouldn't have the heart to do it for anything short of murder."

"Well then, at least there's something to be said for the way I've dumped myself on you, because you won't be alone here if that man comes back. And in a couple of days we'll be abroad--unless," Tessa added, "you change your mind about wanting me to come with you. You'd tell me if you'd sooner I didn't come, wouldn't you?"

Antonia leaned forward and kissed her. She was startled to find that in spite of Tessa's calm voice, her face was feverishly hot. "I shan't change my mind, but I can't help hoping that perhaps you'll change yours," she said.

A tremor went through the girl's body.

"I wonder if you would if you knew the whole story," she said. "You aren't one of the people who think one ought to stick to one's husband at any price, are you? Literally, I mean, at *any* price?"

"Possibly some husbands."

But one of the most difficult problems for Antonia just then was that she hardly knew Tessa's husband. He had always seemed to be very much in love with Tessa, and Roger had a considerable regard for his intelligence, which was not the case with the husbands of any of his other nieces, so Antonia had always been ready to assume that she liked the young man. However, she would have worked at liking Tessa's husband whatever sort of man he had been. The truth was that she knew next to nothing about what went on under cover of his black-browed seriousness and the shyness, if that was what it was, that kept him almost silent when she and Roger were there.

"If only I knew a little more . . ." she began.

At once Tessa stiffened.

"Please, not now," she said, "I'm . . . Oh, I'm so tired, Antonia!" She dropped her head on to her arms. "I can't talk, I can't think. I haven't slept for more than an hour or two for nights. It's funny, I always used to think it was quite easy to make up one's mind and I've always got irritated with the people who didn't seem able to manage it.

But these last weeks . . . Still, it's done now, and there's a sort of peace in it. But I don't think I've ever felt so tired."

"So it's been going on for weeks, whatever it is," Antonia said.

"It's been going on from the beginning, only at first I didn't know what it meant." Tessa lifted her head again, frowning at nothingness, tracking down some desolate thought. "Oh well," she said and was silent for a moment. "But tomorrow we'll go and fix up these tickets, won't we? Then when we're in Greece I can send Alec a picture post-card to tell him where I am. I don't want him to think I've drowned myself, or gone off with another man, or anything like that. I don't want him to worry."

"Oh, you don't?"

As soon as she had said it, Antonia regretted the irony in her voice, but Tessa did not seem to notice it. She only shook her head and answered, "No, of course not."

Antonia herself hoped that Alec would worry a good deal, or at least enough to come to the house that evening, although Tessa, before she went up to bed, tried to make her promise not to let him in if he came. Antonia would only go so far as to agree that she would not let him disturb Tessa that night, and long after Tessa had gone up-stairs, she waited up, reading her detective story inattentively and in snatches, listening for the doorbell to ring. It was midnight before she gave Alec up and went to bed herself.

She slept badly, dreaming that the doorbell kept ringing and that she was afraid to answer it, because she knew that when she did it would not be Alec whom she would find there, but the man in the brown suit, with his long, thin fingers ready to clutch at her like claws. She woke very early with an intense longing to call Roger immediately to reassure herself that he would come home if she needed him. But of course he would and then he would ask her what all the fuss had been about. Putting the temptation from her, she lay watching the movement of a shaft of sunlight across the ceiling, going over in her mind all the things that she still had to do before she left for Greece next day.

She still had to buy the various pills that she liked to take with her whenever she traveled. She wanted some color film too. It was so expensive in Greece. And she must remember to stop the milk and newspapers. That was important. She certainly didn't want to have them accumulating on the doorstep when there might be an undesirable stranger taking an interest in the house. However, it was just the sort of thing that she was most likely to forget, so probably it would be a good idea to deal with the matter at once. Glad that she had found a reason for getting up, she put on her dressing gown and went downstairs.

She wrote notes to the milkman and the paper boy, asking them to stop deliveries after this morning, and took them to the door. She put the note to the milkman into the neck of the empty milk bottle that had not yet been collected, but she was too late for the paper boy. The morning paper was already on the doorstep. Its headlines caught her eye before she had even stooped to pick it up.

"Railway Strike in France . . . Tourists Advised Not to Travel . . . Thousands Stranded. . . ."

It was in a state of mild shock that she retreated with the newspaper to the kitchen. Yet as she sat down at the table and hurriedly began to read everything that referred to the strike, she was aware of a faint feeling of relief. She was almost certain that she had done wrong in inviting Tessa to travel with her. Last night it had seemed a way of giving the girl a chance to cool down before finally wrecking her marriage, but this morning Antonia was inclined to believe that she had done it at least partly for her own sake, because she was not really as keen on the idea of a holiday alone as she had tried to make out. So the strike was a convenient way out for her.

At the same time she was bitterly disappointed. She had looked forward to this holiday for months, had planned everything meticulously, had bought new clothes, had chosen her reading carefully. And now all her thought, her time and her money were to be wasted. When Tessa, also in her dressing gown, presently wandered into the kitchen, she found Antonia looking at the newspaper with such depression that she asked in surprise, "Hullo, what's the bad news? Has somebody started another war with somebody?"

"No, but somebody would like to, if you mean me," Antonia said, holding the paper out to Tessa. "I imagine there are thousands of people wishing that every French railway worker could be blown up by a bomb. The meanness of it! Why do they always have their blasted strikes just when everyone's going on holiday? Why can't they do it when people don't want to travel? I'm sure it would work far better. They'd be respected for their consideration and be much more likely to get what they wanted."

"I don't believe that's really how strikes work," Tessa said. There were still smudges of strain under her eyes this morning, but some color had come back into her cheeks. She stood reading the newspaper without showing any signs of emotion.

Resentfully Antonia thought, "It's all right for her, she never really meant to come. She's had a good night's sleep and she's going home. And that's fine. I'm delighted. Utterly delighted. But damn it, why can't she show a little sympathy for me? Can't she see how I'm feeling?"

21

Tessa lowered the paper.

"I suppose you wouldn't risk it all the same," she said.

"Risk it?" Antonia exclaimed. "Risk traveling across France during a railway strike? Just how, may I ask? Every bus will be full, the car ferries will be booked to the limit and I'm a little past the age for hitchhiking."

"I was thinking of flying," Tessa said.

"No," Antonia said quickly.

"Why not?"

"No."

"But—"

"I don't like it. I never have. I never shall."

"But there's nothing to be scared of. There really isn't. If you compare the number of deaths in air crashes with the number on the roads, or even in railway accidents, you'd realize it's almost the safest way to travel."

"I'm not in the least scared," Antonia said stiffly. "It just happens that I like trains better."

"Well, now there aren't any trains."

"No, but still . . ."

"You don't want to give in tamely and cancel everything, do you?"

"No, but . . . But we'll never be able to get seats," Antonia said hopefully. "Everyone else will have had the same idea."

"We don't know that till we try. If we go to Farr's, we may find your nice Mr. Borrow can fix us up straightaway. Come on, let's get started. I can be ready in a few minutes."

Tessa darted out of the door and went running upstairs.

The mere sound of her flying footsteps made Antonia feel exhausted. She did not move, except to put her elbows on the table and take her head in her hands.

"I won't do it," she proclaimed to the empty kitchen in

a violent whisper. "I won't be pushed around. I won't be stampeded by that child into doing a lot of things I hate. Oh God, that awful lurch when one leaves one's stomach somewhere up among the stars! And suddenly, like this, without making proper plans first, without having time to get used to the idea . . ."

The front doorbell rang.

"And now this," Antonia thought. "Alec—a scene before breakfast—it's too much! I'm sure Roger and I never did this sort of thing to anybody when we were young."

Making more muttering sounds of anger, she got to her feet and went up the basement stairs to the door.

She found Alec Foley standing so close to it, with his thickset body braced, as if he were ready to push straight past her into the house, that she automatically took a quick step backward.

At the same moment Alec stepped back himself, looking at her confusedly.

"I suppose she's here, isn't she?" he said.

His tone was lifeless and his face was slack and gray, as if he had not slept. It was a square face with strong, rather irregular features and curiously anxious brown eyes under bold eyebrows. He was as neatly dressed as he usually was, in a well-pressed dark gray suit that did not fit him very well and brown shoes which, in spite of the crisis in his life, he had not forgotten to polish that morning.

Antonia answered, "Yes, but I'm not sure if she'll see you, Alec. She's in quite a state."

"It doesn't matter," he said. "She's all right, is she?"

"Yes."

"That's all I wanted to know."

He started to turn away.

"Wait," Antonia said. "You'd better come in."

"But if she won't see me . . ."

"You can have some breakfast." Antonia was beginning to feel as sorry for him as she had the evening before for Tessa. She found it dreadful to think that two creatures as young as they were should have got themselves into a situation like this, a situation strictly for adults only. Not that they themselves were aware of any lack of years and experience. "If necessary you can sit in different rooms and be fed and I'll carry messages backwards and forwards as required." She turned back to the basement stairs.

After a moment Alec followed her down. He stood uneasily just inside the kitchen doorway while she made the coffee, put bacon under the grill and bread into the toaster. He appeared to be watching these actions of hers with strangely close attention, but she saw how vacant his eyes were under his frowning black brows.

Presently he asked, "Has she explained why she did it, Mrs. Winfield?"

"She hasn't told me anything," Antonia replied.

"It's so extraordinary," he said. "I'd agreed to everything she wanted. I don't think she's right, but I understand her feelings. I said to her quite definitely, 'All right, I'll do any damned thing you like.' I made it quite clear that I meant it. She can't have misunderstood me."

"Well, drink some coffee." Antonia filled three cups, pushed one toward him, picked up one of the others and went to the door. "I'll take this up to her and see how she feels about coming down to talk to you."

"Thank you—thank you very much," he said.

It was not quite clear if he was thanking her for the coffee or for acting as emissary to his wife, but it was like him not to forget to say it. It was the kind of thing that he always remembered. He seemed to think that it squared his account, freeing him from any obligation to overcome the hostility which, Antonia was sure, he really felt to Tessa's relations. He had very few relations of his own and those that he had he kept with determination at arm's length. A family was something you preferred to get along without, if you were Alec Foley.

Going slowly up the stairs, trying not to slop the coffee into the saucer, Antonia called, "Tessa, Alec's here." Tessa knew that, of course, but it seemed appropriate to warn her that her moment of decision was at hand. "Will you come down, or do you want . . . ?"

Antonia did not trouble to finish the sentence. She had reached the doorway of the spare bedroom. There was no one in the room.

Tessa was not in the bathroom either.

Standing still at the bedroom door, looking thoughtfully around while she drank the coffee that she had brought upstairs, Antonia saw that Tessa's coat and handbag were missing but that her suitcase was still there, with the things that had been inside it tumbled messily out on the bed and the floor. Tessa had always been incurably untidy. She did not look it. She looked as if she were one of the people who are capable of keeping everything in their lives in its right place. The disorder that she actually spread around her generally came as a surprise to new acquaintances.

Going downstairs again, Antonia said, "I'm very sorry, Alec, but she seems to have gone out."

"I suppose she heard me," he said.

"Well, sit down. I expect she'll be back presently. She's left her suitcase."

"Thank you, but I don't think I'll wait," he said. "It wouldn't do much good. And I've got to get to the office. I suppose she hasn't told you what she intends to do."

"She seems to feel she's got to have some time to think,

25

that's all I know. But you'll stay and eat that!" Antonia slammed a plate down on the table and put a knife and fork beside it. "I won't have it wasted and I hate bacon and eggs for breakfast myself."

He hesitated, then obediently sat down.

"Thank you," he said, "it's very good of you."

But he didn't look very grateful and the way that he bolted the food suggested a desire to get away as quickly as possible, rather than hunger.

"She'll be staying here with you, will she?" he asked.

"I wish I knew," Antonia said. "I was leaving for Greece tomorrow and I suggested she might come with me and she seemed to like the idea, but now there's this railway strike in France, so I don't know what's going to happen."

"I see. Will you tell her, then, if she wants money or her clothes, to let me know? I'll send them on to her."

"Oh, Alec—" Antonia put a hand on his arm and only when she touched him realized that he was trembling with an intense anger which his pride had made him determined to conceal.

Jerking away from her, he thanked her once more, said goodbye abruptly and left.

She gave a deep sigh. She hoped that what she had told him was true, that Tessa would soon be back. But it was just possible, she was afraid, that when Tessa had heard her talking reasonably pleasantly to Alec, the girl had been filled with such distrust that she had gone blindly out and now would go to any lengths to avoid returning.

It was two hours before Tessa reassured her, telephoning from the Underground station at Piccadilly. Her voice was cheerful.

"Everything's all right," she said. "I've fixed it up."

"You've fixed it up?" Antonia cried. "You're going back to him? I'm so glad, Tessa. I'm sure it's best—"

"The plane," Tessa broke in, "to Athens. I've got two seats on the ten-forty tonight."

"Then keep them!" Antonia answered shrilly. "Take Alec, take anyone you like, but count me out!"

"No, listen," Tessa said. "It's a wonderful bit of luck. Mr. Borrow fixed it up for you. You needn't cancel anything. You can go on and do everything you planned, and I can keep out of Alec's way till I've sorted things out in my mind. Did he behave dreadfully this morning?"

"He behaved exceedingly well. He said please and thank you for everything and said if you wanted money or your clothes you were to let him know."

There was a short silence.

Then Tessa remarked, "Of course, you intimidate him terribly. But I'm glad he wasn't difficult. Now about tonight, I think the best thing would be for us to meet at Cromwell Road. I don't think I'll come back to Hampstead in case Alec shows up again."

"I don't think he will, you know. I don't think he'll even follow you to Greece, if that's what you're counting on," Antonia said disagreeably.

There was another silence.

When Tessa spoke next, her voice sounded very remote. "You think I'm awful, don't you? But I can't go back to him. Not now. If you simply hate the idea of my coming with you, though, if you think I'll spoil it for you—"

"Oh, my dear, it isn't that," Antonia said sadly. "All right, Cromwell Road. About nine o'clock, I suppose. I'll pack up your suitcase and bring it."

She put the telephone down.

Oh God, an airplane, she thought with horror. And a night flight at that, with nothing to take her mind off her conviction that the thing was going to explode or crash to the ground in another minute. Because of course she was dreadfully afraid of flying, even if she wouldn't normally admit it. And there would be no hope of sleep, with people huddled around her in grotesque shapes in the half-darkness, with stewards thrusting cups of sickly-tasting tinned orange juice into her hand and with the same stars outside in the black sky that she could see from her bedroom window.

Then she remembered that there was one thing to be said for going away, even by plane. If the man in the brown suit came back, he wouldn't find her.

However, in the light of the morning she found that she was no longer so certain that the man whom she had seen at the window the evening before was the man who had followed her to Farr's, and with her fear of flying on her mind, she somehow forgot to feel afraid that he would come back. And in the evening, when her taxi drove away up the street, she did not look behind her even once to see if he was there.

For this reason she did not see the shabby figure emerge from a patch of shadow near the gate and stand staring after her.

# CHAPTER THREE

       The plane left the airport punctually. It rose smoothly. Seat belts were unfastened and cigarettes were lit.

In that moment of relaxation Antonia suddenly began to think of the man again. She smiled. She had just realized who he was and what he had wanted. And really it was incredible, the state that she had worked herself into over him. For obviously he was simply the husband of one of the women who had been coming to see her at Marriage Guidance, or the lover of one of her Unmarried Mothers; the father of the child, perhaps, or someone who was anxious to marry the girl in spite of her trouble. In any case, all that he had wanted with Antonia was to talk.

Once before she had been followed for this reason. It had ended up with her and the man drinking cup after cup of coffee in a gloomy little espresso bar while he told her a new and quite different version of the story of an unhappy marriage that she had heard from his wife. Whether his version was any nearer to the truth than his wife's Antonia had had no means of knowing, but she had felt very sorry for him and had listened patiently and offered a few calming platitudes, for which he had appeared grateful. It had never entered her mind to be afraid of him.

But that man had plucked up his courage to speak to her almost as soon as he had realized that she had noticed him. He hadn't followed her around all day. . . .

The steward came by, asking passengers if they wanted anything from the bar.

Antonia and Tessa ordered whisky and a little later they nibbled at the limp piece of chicken and the one gherkin that were dumped before each of them on a plastic tray. Then Tessa fell asleep, sitting so straight in the narrow seat that sleep looked impossible, but this was the sleep of exhausted nerves. In the dimness, when the lights had been turned low and the bustle of the stewards had stopped and the roaring of the engines in the night was producing a curious sense of stillness and quiet in the plane, Tessa's lolling head and white face looked as drained of life as if she had been through a severe illness.

The sight touched Antonia's heart. At the same time she gave some pity, from a distance, to the man in brown and regretted that it couldn't be something more useful, like a trip to Greece. For really, she had failed him dreadfully. In Farr's she had only given him a look so frozen and unkind that he had immediately dropped all thought of confiding in her, and later, when he had decided to have another try and had come to her house, all that he had got out of her had been a terrified glare that again had frightened him off.

Antonia did not sleep at all in the plane. But she discovered one advantage in flying by night. She did not have to look down at the Alps, with which, from ground level, she was on fairly friendly terms, but which, from above, had always looked to her like a brutal mouthful of teeth, ready to crunch her to powder and swallow her down, and terrified her worse than all the rest of the journey.

Over Brindisi the plane began to bump a little. The voice of the pilot on the loudspeakers informed the passengers that they'd soon be through the turbulence, but that meanwhile they'd all feel more comfortable, wouldn't they, if they fastened their seat belts.

Antonia jogged Tessa and told her to fasten her belt. Tessa groped for the ends of it and as soon as she had clipped it around her, went to sleep again and did not waken until the stewards began hurrying up and down the aisle, turning on lights and preparing for landing.

She opened her eyes then, reached for Antonia's hand and said, "Well, it wasn't so bad, was it?"

"You slept right through it," Antonia replied, "so how do you know?"

"Didn't you sleep?" Tessa asked.

"Not a wink."

"*Was* it bad, then?"

"Not what you'd call bad, I imagine." Antonia was trying to force her feet back into her shoes. They always swelled when she flew. "It just seems to me such a deplorable way of getting from one place to another. You don't have any feeling at all of being abroad. The airports are all exactly alike. They all give you that repulsive sort of damp chicken to eat. And whatever line you fly by, they all keep as calm and governessy as if they were British. You might just as well have stayed at home."

"Except that you're liable to get to the place you want to go to."

"Ah, but you don't have that wonderful moment when the ship docks and hordes of wild men come pushing and shoving on board, ramming their elbows into your ribs and screaming at you, 'Porteur! Porteur!'—and you say to yourself, *'I'm in France!'* And then there's that amazing meal on the train, with the rather beastly wine, but with that first salad you have made by a Frenchman—"

"A Frenchman who's out on strike, together with all those jolly porters," Tessa reminded her.

"All the same, that's the way to travel, the natural way, as Madame Julie said."

Tessa laughed, giving her up as hopeless.

They landed a little late because of a thunderstorm over Athens. It was still raining when they stepped out of the plane. The night air felt like a hot, wet towel clapped over their faces. As they walked across the tarmac they could feel the heavy raindrops striking them singly and drying almost as soon as they had fallen. Occasional flashes of lightning made the hills near the airport stand out in sudden whiteness against the night sky.

When they had passed through customs, Tessa tried to shepherd Antonia to the airport bus, but Antonia, at last asserting herself successfully, hailed a taxi.

Giving the driver the name of her usual hotel, she went on, "You realize, don't you, Tessa, I haven't a room booked for tonight? We're arriving several days too early."

"That's all right, they won't be full up," Tessa said. "It isn't the busy season."

"Oh?" Antonia said. "You seem to know an awful lot about it all of a sudden."

"It's what your Mr. Borrow told me. He said it's much too hot for most people."

"Perhaps it'll be too hot for you then. If it is, don't blame me. And remember, from now on we carry out *my* plans *my* way."

But as Antonia spoke, her irritability mysteriously died. For the fact that the pink-starred bushes by the roadside, across which the headlights glanced, were oleanders and

32

that the gently stirring dark water beyond them was the Gulf of Aegina had just dawned fully on her tired mind. Her nervous system to some extent still resisted the knowledge. It had all come too soon, too abruptly, and not in the way that she was used to, but still the tension went out of her and she yawned with contentment.

"Ah well, we're here," she said. "I expect I'll be nicer about it tomorrow."

Tessa answered with an absent smile. She was leaning forward in her seat, looking out of the window. There was nothing much to be seen but the empty road and the scattered commonplace buildings of any seashore, and ahead were the denser lights of a city that could have been any city in the world. Yet there was the stillness of a deep excitement on her face.

Antonia thought, "It's got her already, it's beginning, the Greek dream. . . . But thank God, I don't think she'll start quoting things at me." Opening her handbag, she gave her attention to remembering the value in pounds and shillings of the drachmas that she had been given at Farr's.

The hotel to which they were driven was in a side street off Omonia Square and was a modest place, but comfortable, except for continuously murmurous plumbing. They had no difficulty in obtaining a room, and once Antonia was in bed the water pipes could have shouted and argued with one another, like Athenians in the street, without keeping her awake.

She woke when a bar of sunlight, filtering through the Venetian blinds, fell across her face. The first thing that she was aware of as she blinked her eyes against the unfamiliar brilliance was the already fairly oppressive heat of the morning. The next was the tremendous din of voices and traffic, helped out by an electric drill at work somewhere near at hand. Then she became aware that she was alone in the room. The bed in which Tessa had gone to sleep was a tumbled mess of bedclothes, her belongings lay scattered on the floor around her open suitcase, but Tessa herself was not there.

On the dressing table, however, propped against the looking glass, was a piece of paper with something written on it. Antonia got out of bed and crossed the room to read it. The note said, "Have gone sightseeing on my own, as you told me. Don't bother about me."

Which was all very well and probably well meant, Antonia thought, as she picked up the telephone and ordered breakfast for herself, but it would have been better if Tessa had told her just for how long she was not to bother. Until lunchtime? Until dinner? When were they supposed to see each other again?

Not that it mattered much. In spite of her long sleep, Antonia's head was still muzzy with fatigue and she had no wish to go anywhere or do anything that day.

But she had often noticed what a disastrous thing it seemed to be to make plans to do nothing. You wouldn't think that it was an excessive thing to demand just occasionally, yet it was always when you had most set your heart on doing nothing at all, had given your mind to obtaining it, that something seemed bound to go wrong. So even if nothing could go seriously wrong on the island when she eventually got there, since it was practically without roads, had only two cars and one bus, no television, no cinema, no antiquities to bring sightseers and only three thousand inhabitants and three policemen, it might be as well to approach today with caution.

But in fact nothing went wrong that day. Antonia's breakfast arrived, she had a shower and presently, in a

34

dress that she had bought the year before from Madame Julie, a bold yellow and white stripe, and with dark glasses and a scarf over her head, she set out to send a telegram to Roger.

It took her a little while to compose, for she had not made up her mind how much to tell him about Tessa. In the end she wrote: "Came to Athens by air otherwise proceeding as planned except have brought Tessa for holiday from Alec whom I suggest you contact love Antonia."

After that she strolled along Stadiou Street and bought a shady straw hat and a pair of attractive sandals. The humidity of the night had gone, but the day heat was harsh and exhausting. Beginning to pant a little and thinking with some dismay of perhaps having to spend some days in Athens, instead of the single night of her original plan, she went to a restaurant where she remembered that there was air-conditioning, ate delicious lobster, then took a taxi back to her hotel and, in the relative quiet of the siesta time, went to sleep again.

When she awoke, she had another shower, dressed, and thinking that Tessa would surely appear at any moment now, wrote on a piece of paper, "Look for me in the bar," propped it against the looking glass as Tessa had in the morning, tucked a book under her arm and went downstairs.

There was no one in the bar as yet but the elderly, multilingual bartender and a youngish man in a red sports shirt who was sitting on one of the high stools with his head in his hands.

When he heard Antonia order Scotch and soda, he raised his head, stared at her for a moment with a look of vacant melancholy, then exclaimed, "Madam, you speak English!"

From the solemnity of his voice and the degree of surprise in it, considering that in that particular hotel almost no language but English was ever spoken, Antonia deduced that he was at least moderately drunk.

"Yes, I do," she answered equably and was turning away to sit down in a comfortable chair by the open window when he spoke again.

"Madam, I apologize for intruding upon you, but if you'll permit me, I'd like to give you this flower." From a corsage of pink and white carnations, tied with white satin ribbon, which lay before him on the bar, he dragged a pink carnation and held it out to her. "I should like very much to give a flower to somebody, just a single flower, and you speak English."

There was a trace of Glasgow in his own speech. He had fair, curly hair and a round, red, sweating face.

"Thank you," Antonia said, taking the flower and again starting off for a chair.

"Thank you for accepting it," he answered gravely. "Please wear it."

Antonia obligingly fastened it to her dress with her brooch.

"Thank you," he said again. "It helps to see somebody do that. Would you believe it, I became engaged to be married today and do you know where my fiancée is? She's sitting out there in the lobby by herself. She's been sitting there all alone for the last hour."

"Then why don't you go and join her?" Antonia asked.

"Because she said she would join me here," he said. "An hour ago she said that. 'Go in and order drinks for us,' she said. 'I must wait here for my friend.' So I came here and I ordered three gin-and-tonics, one for her, one for me, one for her friend. I drank mine and I ordered another. And I took my time about it—didn't I, Joe?" he appealed to the bartender.

"You ordered another three, sir," the bartender said.

The other man nodded. "That's right, I saw the ice begin to melt and I thought, 'That won't do for my girl and her friend, whoever she is.' And I thought, 'Who is she, this friend? That's something I ought to know when I'm buying drinks for her.' But they all have friends, these girls. They're always waiting for one another, and going to visit one another, and talking about one another. But today we became engaged to be married, so you'd think we could get along without the friend for once. Don't you think so?"

"Haven't you been out to see why she's taking so long?" Antonia asked.

"Oh yes, and there she sat by the door like an image and she said, 'Go in and order drinks for us. I must wait here for my friend.' And it isn't as if she doesn't like it here. She said this was where she wanted to come because it's quiet. Quiet! Here I've sat with no one to talk to but Joe till you arrived, madam. Not that I've a thing against Joe. He's a friend, he's done his best, telling me about his travels round the world when he was a cabin boy on a sailing ship. Round and round the world he went, having adventure after adventure. But that was a good while ago, as it happens, and I think I've heard it all before some other time."

"Perhaps if you'd actually given her the flowers . . ."

"I did, I did," he cried. "And she said, 'I can't wear them sitting here by myself, waiting for my friend, everyone would look at me.' She said, 'Take them away with you and order drinks for us. . . .'"

Antonia had given up the idea of trying to read. She hitched herself onto one of the bar stools.

"Is your fiancée English?" she asked.

"No, she's Greek," he said. "A beautiful Greek. And

that's part of the trouble. She doesn't actually speak much English. I suppose you don't speak Greek, do you?"

Antonia shook her head. "Strictly phrase book, I'm afraid."

"You see, I come over here quite often from Iran," he said. "I'm an engineer and they give us one week off a month and most of us take it in Malta or Athens. It's cheaper in Malta but the women are more exciting in Athens, if you understand me. I like Athens. But the language is a problem. Half the time we don't understand each other. Perhaps that's the trouble today. What do you think? Do you think I could have misunderstood her?"

"It doesn't seem impossible," Antonia said.

"Ah, but the misunderstanding may not have been on the level of language, that's what you mean, isn't it?" he said with owlish solemnity.

"Why don't you go and ask her how long she means to wait for her friend?" she suggested.

"No," he said. "Definitely no. I'm afraid."

"There can't be anything to be afraid of."

"Oh yes, there can. Very much so. I'm afraid she isn't there at all. Afraid she's gone home. Afraid that's what she meant to do all along. Oh God, I'm afraid! Madam—" He leaned toward Antonia and looked intently into her face. "I apologize very sincerely for inflicting my private troubles on you, but you say you speak some phrases of Greek, so would you please have the kindness—would you please have the very great kindness—to take a look outside yourself and if you see a small girl in a pink dress with white spots sitting like an image near the door, go and ask her how long she means to go on waiting for this friend of hers? Tell her I'm not bored, tell her I'm not impatient, but that I'd just like to know. Would you do that?"

Antonia was about to answer that she didn't mind taking

38

a look outside, if that would reassure him, but that as for questioning an unknown Greek girl on such a matter, she really didn't feel up to it, when a small dark girl in a pink dress with white spots came in at the door.

The man gave a cry of joy, jumped unsteadily to his feet and threw his arms around her.

"And your friend too!" he cried. "She came—your beautiful friend!"

Letting go of the girl, he opened his arms again and threw them as warmly, as eagerly round Tessa, who had come in just behind the other girl.

# CHAPTER FOUR

"No," the Greek girl said stiffly. "That is not my friend."

She was slender and small-boned, with a small, pallid face and dark hair which was smoothly swathed around her head in a tremendous cocoon. She had remarkable dark eyes, almost as large and as fierce as those of the women in the wall paintings of Knossos.

"My friend has telephoned to say she has to go home to her mother," she said. "Her mother is not well. You should beg this lady's pardon for your mistake."

"When I was just thinking she'd been worth waiting for." The man detached another flower from the corsage that he had bought for his fiancée and held it out to Tessa. The rest of it he pushed away from him as if he had lost interest in it. "Madam, please accept this with my most sincere apologies," he said humbly.

Tessa gave Antonia a questioning glance, saw that accepting flowers from this man appeared to be the order of the day, and took the one that she was being offered.

She was starting to say something to Antonia when he

interrupted. "You know each other? Isn't that splendid? Then we're all friends after all and we can have a drink together. Scotch again? Joe, another Scotch for the lady. And you?" he asked Tessa.

She shook her head decisively and said that she and her aunt were just going to have dinner. He protested that they couldn't possibly dine as early as this in Athens, but they made for the door, leaving him and his fiancée to their problems.

The dining room was empty except for a party of American women who were arguing about whether or not it would be too hot to go to Delphi next day.

Sitting down, Tessa asked Antonia, "What was all that about, and how did you get involved?"

"What I *think* it was about," Antonia said, "is that the girl was keeping him waiting because she was hoping for a phone call from a better prospect. And the man, when he gets himself sufficiently drunk, likes to persuade himself he's engaged to the girl of the moment and that everything between them is very fine and respectable, just as his Presbyterian parents would like it to be. I expect when he's sober he doesn't worry so much. But perhaps I'm doing them both a wrong. Now tell me what you've been doing all day. Have you been to the Acropolis?"

"Yes, naturally—and please don't, don't say, 'Of course those awful crowds completely spoil it,' because nothing could, and anyway they belong there. It was always meant to be jam-packed with a lot of people, wasn't it? And to dominate everything all the same. What have you been doing?"

"Sleeping, mostly. Have you sent that picture postcard to Alec?"

"No, I haven't done that yet. But I did something else. I went along to Farr's agent and asked, since we'd arrived several days early, if we could leave for the island a bit early too. And they said we could leave tomorrow, if we liked, but that otherwise we'd have to wait till next Monday, when you meant to go anyway, because there are only two sailings a week. So I fixed up for us to go tomorrow, subject to confirmation by telephone this evening. What do you think? Shall we go?"

"Why not?—though in a way I'm surprised you want to leave so quickly," Antonia said. "The first time I came to Athens I didn't know how to tear myself away."

She thought that Tessa's clear gaze became evasive.

"I thought you'd probably prefer it," she said. "But if you don't, I can ring up and tell them so."

"Oh, I'll be very glad to go," Antonia replied. "But I've an idea your real reason for wanting to move on is that then there'll be less temptation to jump on a plane and go straight home again."

"Something like that, perhaps," Tessa admitted. "There *is* a temptation."

"Then why not simply go, my dear?"

"No, don't let's start that again. It wouldn't help. But that doesn't mean that staying away is going to be quite as easy as I thought."

"And it wouldn't help either to tell me just a little about what's gone wrong?"

"Well, if you want to know . . . I suppose, in a sense, you could say it's all political."

"I thought you and Alec agreed about all that sort of thing," Antonia said. "You both always sound very anti-bomb and you went on one of those Aldermaston marches together, didn't you?"

"Oh, that. That was just a phase." Tessa made it sound like one of the follies of extreme youth, remembered with a mixture of tenderness and embarrassment. "You know

how it is in the spring. 'So priketh him natur in hir corages,
Than longen folks to gone on pilgrimages. . . .' "

"Then where do the politics come in?" Antonia asked.

"I'm sorry, they don't. I was just talking nonsense."
Turning from her to the waiter with one of her brightest
smiles, Tessa began to consult him about all the incomprehensible names on the menu.

By the time the meal had been ordered, Antonia had decided that it was not worthwhile to persevere in trying to
draw confidences from Tessa before she was ready to give
them without persuasion.

Since they had decided to leave Athens next day, and
as this meant that they must be at the bus station at seven
o'clock, Antonia arranged after dinner to be called very
early. For there was nothing that she hated like a hurried
start. She liked to have time to dress carefully and repack
properly, to check all the documents in her handbag and
make sure that she was leaving nothing behind. But for
Tessa getting up was always a last-minute business. So
next morning Antonia's pleasant feeling of being dressed
in plenty of time, of being well organized and well prepared for the day ahead, was all but destroyed right
at the very beginning by the certainty that they were going to miss the bus. Yet, once Tessa had been persuaded to
wake up, she somehow succeeded in getting out of bed,
jamming her mess of clothes back into her suitcase, drinking a cup of coffee and being ready to leave, all in about
ten minutes. She managed to look reasonably well
groomed too, in a sleeveless cotton dress and bright-
colored sandals and with her fair hair well brushed and
shining.

They took a taxi to the bus station. Antonia had put on
her new blue and green dress with the gilded belt, but was
vaguely dissatisfied with it, she did not know why. She

43

wished that Roger had had a chance to see it before he left for Edinburgh and to tell her what he thought of it. Not that he was any expert on clothes, but when she had wrung a favorable opinion out of him, even an absent-minded one, it always fortified her.

In the bus station she and Tessa joined the group of people who were waiting for the bus which would take them to the port fifty miles north of Athens, from which the ship would leave for the island.

An empty bus for the place was waiting there in the bus station, but no one was being allowed to get in, while a man standing on top of the bus and two men on the ground shouted at one another in an argument of the kind that precedes the departure of almost any vehicle in Greece, and a pretty girl in a short, tight dress and gold sandals trotted busily around among the waiting people, checking their names against a list that she held.

Coming up to Antonia and Tessa, she said in excellent English, "Mrs. Winfield? Mrs. Foley? I am your guide. Anything you want to know, please ask me. Now you must not get in this bus, you must get in the other one."

At the moment there was no sign of another bus, but the one around which they were all waiting suddenly began to move and, with the man on the roof still shouting and gesticulating, drove rapidly out of the bus station.

"It looks as if we're going to have a late start," Antonia observed to Tessa.

A tall, white-haired man standing nearby overheard and reassured them. "You'll see, we'll go out right on time. They allow for all the kefuffle in their schedule."

He was rather plump, with long, plump, pink cheeks and light blue eyes under bushy dark eyebrows. His loose gray suit was not of English cut, but there was no trace of a foreign accent in his English.

He went on, "Sometimes it seems to me as if all Greeks live in a continuous state of frantic anxiety and I find it's very important not to be infected by it, because our own nervous systems simply won't stand the strain. But it suits them and they thrive on it."

"*Saloniki! Saloniki!*" shouted a barefooted boy at Antonia, thrusting a tray of fresh rolls into her middle and raising his voice with the desperate insistence of the Athenian child who has been sent out to sell something. "*Saloniki! Saloniki!*"

When she shook her head, the boy shouted again and was plainly prepared to go on and on until she weakened, but the white-haired man spoke sharply to him in Greek, at which the boy shrugged and retreated, to start shouting at two men nearby who were conversing quietly in German.

"Noise—that's another thing they thrive on, like all Mediterranean peoples," the white-haired man said. "The Northern races for some reason coddle their nerves against noise. I confess I don't understand the apparent correlation with climate. Not that I've explored the subject thoroughly. I've never, for instance, investigated the volume of sound that's acceptable to an Eskimo."

Just then an increase of noise, a swelling wave of shouting, heralded the arrival of another bus. Behind it came two more, and as they backed, one after the other, into the bus station, a dozen people shrieked excited advice to the drivers, as if they did not execute this maneuver every morning of their lives.

The guide came running up to Antonia and Tessa.

"Mrs. Winfield, Mrs. Foley, please come with me, you are in the first bus," she cried.

Hustling them onto it, she placed a middle-aged American couple in the two seats behind them and the two

45

Germans across the aisle, and then hurried on to place the other passengers. Everything now was done at extreme speed and when the bus drove off, with the luggage lashed on top, it was a mere minute or two late, as the white-haired man had predicted.

At that time the morning was still fresh and cool, the sky was a hazy blue and the arid hills had not yet begun to shimmer with the menacing glitter of heat.

The first part of the journey was along a modern high-way, then along a narrower road through the hills, passing occasional white villages where women, many of them with veiled faces, came to their doorways to watch the buses go by.

As soon as the guide had made sure that her flock had settled themselves, she sat down on a seat beside the driver, opened a large handbag, took out a hunk of bread and began to munch it. When she had finished it she brought out another hunk, then another. Continuously, until the first halt on the journey—a sprawling, red-roofed village where the buses were driven onto a ferryboat, to be transported across a narrow inlet of the sea, then go on by road—she went on eating the heavy, yellowish bread.

The sun was very hot now and the sea was a burning blue. A strong scent of eucalyptus from the trees on the shore was mixed with the pungent odors of meat grilling on charcoal. As soon as the buses stopped, shrill shouting sprang up to help them onto the ferryboat, but first a donkey cart had to be driven on board. The cart was brilliantly painted with flowery wreaths and garlands, the donkey's harness braided and tasseled in bright colors. The man who led it wore baggy black trousers, felt leggings and a wide sash, and the horde of children who had stayed in the cart made a fluttering heap there of pinks, reds, greens and yellows, like a crate of brilliant birds.

When the boat moved away from the shore, Antonia and Tessa, who had got out of the buses with the other passengers, went into the small refreshment room and ordered bread and cheese and beer. Afterward they went to sit on the deck in the shade of an awning, but Tessa soon grew restless and wandered away. Antonia, staying where she was, watched the approaching shore and the people near her.

She saw the white-haired man who had spoken to them at the bus station walking up and down, fanning himself with a magazine and pausing now and then to speak to the people he passed. She could not tell if he did this because he was acquainted with them or because he always talked to anyone who happened to be within reach.

She saw the two Germans, one short and square-headed, with a puffy child's face above a middle-aged body, the other huge and blond and with massive jaws constantly rolling as he masticated a thick salami sandwich. Standing side by side at the rail, they conversed perpetually, deeply interested in one another and in nothing else.

She saw the middle-aged American couple, who had sat behind her and Tessa on the bus, taking photographs of everything in sight, and another American, a solitary young man with a shy, pink and white, very good-looking face, who wore a dirty white shirt and old jeans and stood still and relaxed in a dream.

Antonia also saw a short, fat Greek taking care of his wife and a large family of young girl-children, all brown and beautiful. She saw him trying to keep them all together in one place, trying to keep count of them, trying to keep them quiet, and laughing with a sort of exasperated pride in their adventurousness and cunning when one of them vanished away among the legs and parcels of the other passengers. When he noticed Antonia watching the children, he gave her a glowing smile which invited her to share for the moment in his delight in his family.

She smiled back. She felt wonderfully at peace with herself and grateful to Tessa for having made her come to Greece in spite of the railway strike in France. Then all at once she realized that the ferryboat had almost reached the farther shore and that Tessa had not returned.

She got up and went in search of her. After a few minutes she found her on the small upper deck. She was talking to a man. He was tall, slender, dark, wore jeans and a loudly checked shirt. They both had their backs turned to Antonia. She spoke and they turned. The man had thin, sharp features, wary black eyes and a peak of hair growing low on his forehead.

At Antonia's exclamation, Tessa's hand shot out to grasp her arm.

"What's wrong—are you ill?" she asked.

The man murmured something and moved away.

Antonia could not bring herself to look after him. She stared blindly at the glittering sea.

"Who's that man?" she asked in a whisper. "Where did he come from?"

"He was on one of the buses, I suppose," Tessa said. "He came up here soon after I did and we started talking."

"What about?"

"Oh, nothing special."

"What?" Antonia insisted. "*What* were you talking about?"

Tessa looked into her face with increasing bewilderment.

"As a matter of fact," she said, "we were talking about that thing the American archaeologists built in the Agora in Athens. He was saying it stuck out like a sore thumb and spoilt the whole place and I was saying that for someone as ignorant as I am it's a help to understanding what some of these places were like before they turned into interesting ruins."

"Oh, so he isn't ignorant himself, he knows all about such things!"

Tessa waited before she spoke, then asked quietly, "What's the trouble, Antonia? You aren't worrying because a man tried to pick me up, are you?"

"It's that he tried to pick *you* up! It's that he's here at all! Because he's that man I told you about, the one who followed me about in London."

Tessa did not answer at all this time.

Antonia thought desperately, "Oh God, she thinks I've gone stark crazy. And perhaps I have. Perhaps I have!"

She turned her head to take a careful look at the man and assure herself that he really was the one who had followed her in London. But he had gone. There was no one up here with her and Tessa but the fat little Greek and one of his daughters, whom he was trying to capture before the ferryboat reached the shore and who was fleeing before him with squeals of happiness.

Antonia saw the man in the checked shirt briefly again as the passengers trooped off the boat and climbed back into their buses. He was some distance ahead and she saw only the back of his dark head and his stooping shoulders, which struck her as looking wider and stronger in the loose shirt than they had in his tight brown suit, but not essentially different. Oh no, not different!

She did not speak of him again to Tessa for some time after the bus had started. Tessa did not speak either, but looked straight ahead with a frown creasing her forehead.

After a while Antonia said, "Listen, Tessa, I know what

you're thinking, but you're quite wrong. It *is* the same man. You may find it's harder to believe that than that I've gone mad, but I don't. I don't think I'm mad."

Tessa reached for her hand and held it. "But why—why's he here?"

"Yesterday I thought I'd found the explanation," Antonia said. "I thought of it in the plane and it seemed reasonable so long as he'd just been following me about in London. I thought he must be the husband of one of my cases at Marriage Guidance, or something of that sort, and that he wanted to talk to me but couldn't face going openly to the office. It happened like that once before. But if that was who he was, he'd hardly have followed me to Greece, would he!"

"No," Tessa said.

"But there's no other explanation I can think of—unless he's got me mixed up with somebody else."

"I suppose that's possible," Tessa said unwillingly.

Antonia realized she still did not believe it was the same man and, that being so, she must believe that Antonia's imagination, to say the least, was rather dangerously inflamed. In the circumstances it was stupid to go on talking about him. Yet Antonia could not resist it.

"What was he like to talk to?" she asked. "What sort of man was he?"

"Oh, quite ordinary," Tessa said.

"How did he speak? What sort of accent had he?"

"Just ordinary."

"For God's sake, you know there's no such thing as an ordinary English accent! There are hundreds of them. Thousands, probably."

"Well then, a rather—stagey sort of accent, I suppose you might call it. I shouldn't be surprised if he's an actor."

"What were his fingernails like? Were they black?"

"I didn't notice. And I should have, you know, if they had been. It's a thing one does notice. So do stop worrying, Antonia. It can't possibly be the same man."

"He could have cleaned his nails," Antonia muttered, but when Tessa did not reply to that she abandoned the argument.

But she did not abandon her conviction that the man was the one who had followed her and when later she saw him on the quay, and then again on the ship, and was able to give him a long, deliberate look as he strolled about, her certainty of his identity grew even stronger. It was true that he had cleaned himself up a certain amount since she had seen him last and that his change of clothes had made him look rather less as if he had just crawled out from under a stone with a fierce grudge against the daylight. But the nervous features were the same, and so was the look of strain about them, and so were the hands with which he kept lighting his eternal cigarettes. Positively he was the same man, and positively it could be no coincidence that he was here. He had followed her.

The certainty had an unexpectedly calming effect on her. She went on watching him. He was talking to one of the stewards now, and although they were too far away for Antonia to overhear what they were saying, it occurred to her as she watched the movement of their lips that they were talking in Greek. She wasn't sure of it. She had heard that steward talking fluent English. And it wouldn't necessarily make things any more fantastic than they already were if it turned out that they were speaking in Arabic or Hindustani. But it added to the interest of the situation. For if she was right, then the man must have known all along that she was coming to Greece, must have been chosen to follow her *because* he spoke Greek. . . .

51

What was she saying? Who had chosen him to follow her? Or rather, who had chosen him to follow—some other woman? Because that had to be the explanation of why he was here. It was the only possible explanation. He was following the wrong woman. And that was a very unpleasant thought. For if to this man she was not Antonia Winfield, the middle-aged and entirely respectable wife of a middle-aged and equally respectable professor of marine biology now happily fishing in Scotland, then the whole reassurance that there was in the thought of being Antonia Winfield, whom no one had any reason to spy on, to rob or to murder, disappeared. A whole world of unfamiliar dangers opened up before her. Anything could happen.

# CHAPTER FIVE

And there ahead was the island where, because it had no roads to speak of and only one or two cars, no television, no cinema, a mere three thousand inhabitants and only three policemen, nothing could possibly happen. . . .

Antonia watched it rising out of the sea, at first only a blue blur on the horizon, which presently took on the spiny outline of a prehistoric reptile, drowsily afloat on the shining water, then grew up into a group of mountains, still wrapped about in a blue haze. The ship was quite close to the island before these emerged as rugged but not very high, with the vivid green of the Mediterranean pine covering their lower slopes and a narrow inlet of the sea winding in between two promontories to a small harbor.

The harbor was so small that the ship had to anchor some distance out, while two motor launches came to meet it and pick up the passengers. Luggage and passengers together were crammed into the launches, which, when they made off for the shore, were loaded so heavily and unevenly that Antonia half expected to be submerged at any moment. But they reached the quay safely, where the two taxis of the island and also an ancient bus were waiting.

All the way to the shore Antonia had kept a hopeful eye on the taxis, but the tall, white-haired man reached one of them before anyone else and was whisked away in it, and the other had been booked in advance for the short Greek and his large family. Tessa and Antonia once more had to join the throng of people waiting for the bus.

Already an apparently murderous argument had developed between a man standing on its roof, who was starting to haul the luggage up and lash it there, and a man on the ground, who was in charge of the largest and oldest weighing machine that Antonia had ever seen, and who seemed to be demanding that he should be allowed to weigh the luggage before it was stacked on top of the bus. He was large and old himself, with a massive paunch hanging out over the top of his cotton trousers and a two-day growth of grizzled beard on his chin. When no one took any notice of him, his voice developed a note of thunderous fury. The words he used were nowhere in Antonia's phrase book, but she was able to guess the sense of a good many of them. Still nobody took any notice of him.

Suddenly he could stand it no longer. Thrusting himself forward and confronting the middle-aged American, who was just about to hand his luggage up to the man on top of the bus, the other snatched the cases and with a cry of triumph dumped them on his weighing machine.

The American stared at him for a moment in silent consternation. Then like a paper bag explosively disintegrating and spilling its contents in all directions, his American personality split at all its seams and out poured Greek. Everything about him became Greek, his gestures, his volubility, his zest in making a scene.

His wife stood placidly watching as he fought to prevent his luggage being weighed. There was no obvious reason why he should have feared its being weighed, since it was plainly no heavier or bulkier than that of anyone else, but he appeared to be moved by a passionate feeling that he had been singled out most unjustly, was being disgracefully discriminated against.

Most of the other people waiting to get on to the bus, who were natives of the island, returning home after a visit to the mainland, listened with patience and appreciation. But the shy-looking young American moved away to a slight distance, very pink in the face, and fixed a look of embarrassed apology on a mountain top. Why did this sort of thing always have to happen, he seemed to be asking, when you ran across your compatriots abroad? Why was it always this kind that got around?

Meanwhile, the shorter, square-headed German turned with a questioning look to the Englishman, if that was what he was, in the checked shirt, who nodded back with understanding, and between them they unobtrusively handed up all the remaining luggage to the man on top of the bus. It had all been tied down and the passengers had got into the bus before the argument over the weighing of the American's suitcases had come to an end.

But all at once the man with the weighing machine seemed to feel that he had stood up sufficiently for himself and the dignity of his machine and lost interest in the whole matter. The other as suddenly became an American again and as he helped his wife on to the bus and followed her to a seat, said with a self-conscious air, "Sorry, folks, I don't often do that, but when I do, I sure make it good."

The bus started.

It took a quarter of an hour to reach the hotel, along a narrow road between low, scrub-covered hills. The hotel was a long white building on the shore of a small bay, with a cluster of small white houses near it and a few more houses dotted along the curving sweep of sand dunes which ended at a squat, stone windmill. But most of the village was on the hill that rose steeply behind the hotel, crowned by some jagged rocks.

Antonia was given a room on the upper floor of the hotel. Tessa's was on the lower. Each had a private shower and a balcony facing the sea. Antonia unpacked at once, arranging her belongings methodically for the three weeks ahead. But when she went downstairs to Tessa's room, she found that Tessa was sitting on the edge of the bed, gazing expressionlessly out at the glittering Aegean, and had not even opened her suitcase. There were the marks of tears on her cheeks.

Antonia wanted to take her in her arms and comfort her. But remembering her resolution not to probe again for confidences, she only remarked, as she paused halfway across the room to look at herself in the long mirror, "I sometimes feel like that too. I suddenly start thinking how much more I'd like it if only Roger would come with me, instead of going off after those miserable salmon. I've sometimes thought of faking a desperate illness or something to get him here just once, because then I think he'd quite likely want to come again. . . . Tessa, what's wrong with this dress? I was so pleased with it when I bought it, but now I don't seem to care for it much."

Tessa turned her head, brushing the traces of her tears away with her hand. She looked critically at Antonia.

"It's the belt," she said.

"Yes, that's what I was beginning to think," Antonia said. "It's too broad, or something. And the buckle's too big and clumsy. Yet I liked it when I tried it on. Perhaps it's the difference between seeing it in a fitting room, when it doesn't worry you that you look as if you were going to a party, and seeing it out in the light of day. But I'm not the right shape to wear the dress without the belt, so I suppose I'll have to put up with it as it is, unless I can buy a plain white one in one of the shops here. Perhaps I'll go out later and see if I can."

"Just a minute, I've an idea," Tessa said and stood up, opened her suitcase and started throwing her clothes out onto the floor. "It's somewhere here. . . . I'm sure I put it in. . . . Yes, here it is." She extracted something from the inside of a shoe and held it out to Antonia. "Try it on and see how it looks," she said.

It was a narrow belt made of what looked like small gold coins, joined by fine gold chains and with a delicate clasp made from two larger coins, stamped with the austere profile of some goddess.

Antonia took off the heavy leather belt and fastened the other around her waist.

"Oh, it's charming!" she exclaimed. "I do like it, Tessa. What is it? Where did you get it?"

"Yes, it's a great improvement," Tessa said. "We found it in a junk shop one day. It isn't anything special."

"But you'll want to wear it yourself," Antonia said and started to undo the clasp.

"No, keep it," Tessa said quickly. "I mean, keep it altogether, if you like it. I know I shan't wear it. I don't really know why I packed it."

"Thank you—but I'll just borrow it for the present," said Antonia, to whom it was obvious enough both why Tessa had packed the belt and why she now felt incapable of wearing it. It was simply because she and Alec had chosen it together. "Now let's see if we can get something to eat.

That bread and cheese we had on the ferry doesn't seem to have lasted very well."

They had a lunch of grilled mullet, roast chicken, salad, apricots and some Spata rosé.

Because it was after two o'clock, the dining room was empty except for the other people who had arrived on the bus, the two Germans, the young American, the middle-aged American couple and the man in the checked shirt. He was already sitting at a corner table when Antonia and Tessa came in. He looked bored and listless and was biting one of his newly scrubbed nails.

Neither the white-haired man nor the Greek with the large family appeared to be staying in the hotel, but later in the day, after a siesta, a lazy swim and an hour of sunning themselves on the beach, Antonia and Tessa encountered both of them again. They met the white-haired man coming out of a little shop in the hotel to which they had gone to buy cigarettes.

Smiling with pleasure at seeing them, as if they were old friends whom he was unexpectedly meeting in this remote place, he said, "Ah, there you are! Comfortably settled in, I hope."

He was carrying a string bag full of fruit and vegetables and was clutching a loaf of bread under one arm. He had changed out of his foreign-looking suit into a short-sleeved, navy blue shirt, well-cut white cotton shorts and rope-soled shoes, and looked younger and more muscular than he had on the journey from Athens.

"I hope you find the hotel satisfactory," he went on. "The food isn't at all bad, is it, as Greek food goes? I sometimes eat there myself. But cooking for myself is one of my pleasures here. The local produce is so delicious. One can practically live on the fish and the fruit. Perhaps you'll drop in sometime and sample my efforts. Or come at least for a drink. I live in the last house before you get to the windmill. My name, by the way, is Mobey—Sam Mobey. I know your names. News travels fast on an island. And I've been wondering, Mrs. Winfield, if you're any relation of Professor Winfield—Roger Winfield."

"He's my husband," Antonia said.

Mr. Mobey beamed. "Isn't that amazing? I always say it's practically impossible to meet anyone anywhere without discovering a mutual acquaintance. Not that I can claim personal acquaintance with your distinguished husband, Mrs. Winfield, but I can with some of his work. I have interests of my own that tend in the same direction —purely amateur, I'm afraid, but still I read all that I can in his field. So that's all the more reason, isn't it, why you should honor me with a visit? Any time you happen to be passing. I'm nearly always at home. I'd be so very delighted if you would." He gave a little bow and was about to walk on when he paused and added, "And if you'll forgive my saying so, what a very charming belt that is you're wearing. A very nice free rendering of some famous pieces, most cleverly executed. I take a certain interest in numismatics too, you see. But there—what a dabbler you'll think me, and indeed, how right you'll be!"

He laughed and strode off, but almost at once stopped again to talk to the next person he met.

Antonia and Tessa went into the shop and bought cigarettes, then strolled on in the pleasant coolness of the late afternoon along a narrow, dusty track that ran parallel with the shore behind the houses on the sand dunes. The houses were flat-roofed and single-storied, with trellises over their doorways, smothered in vines and, wherever there was room for them to stand in the small gardens, big brown earthenware pots with carnations, canna lilies, basil and geraniums growing in them. As Antonia and Tessa were passing one of these houses, an old woman, all in black, with gray plaits hanging down each side of her face, darted out suddenly into their path and, with a soft greeting, thrust a bunch of marigolds into Tessa's hand; almost before Tessa could gasp thank you, she had vanished back through her door. It was while they were still standing there, startled and moved by the unexpectedness and grace of the old woman's gesture and the beauty of her toothless smile, that the short Greek of the many daughters hailed them.

For a horrible moment as Antonia looked toward him, she thought that the hand with which he was beckoning to them from the shade of a large mulberry tree was covered in blood. Certainly something thick and red was smeared all over his plump fingers and had trickled in crimson streaks down his bare forearm to his elbow. His smiling face, too, was stained with red about the mouth and chin. However, it was not a cannibal meal that he was enjoying, but merely a feast of mulberries.

"You like mulberries?" he said, holding out a bowl. "Please take, but be very careful of your dresses. The stain is bad. To eat mulberries you should dress like me."

He patted his naked paunch, leaving red fingerprints there, and laughed gaily. He had nothing on but swimming trunks, a wide-brimmed straw hat and sunglasses.

As Antonia and Tessa helped themselves from his bowl, he went on, "You like it here? You make holiday? You stay in the hotel? Much better to do as I do. I write to the police, I say I want a house for myself, my wife, my children. I say I want kitchen, shower, toilet, two-three rooms, that is all I need. Then we come here and do as we like and all at logical prices."

"The police?" Antonia said, intrigued. "You write to the police to find you a house?"

"Naturally, it is their duty," he said. "What else should they do here? Very peaceful place, very peaceful people. Have you been upstairs yet?"

It took Antonia a moment to realize that he was asking if they had been up the hill behind the hotel. She said that they had not yet done so.

"Very interesting," he said. "The town at the top is very old. You know why they build up there instead of down here? Many pirates coming, and from upstairs they see them and give warning. There is a nice museum too, you must see, and nice restaurants. You will have a nice holiday. You are staying how long?"

"About three weeks," Antonia answered.

"But not here," he said. "Soon you go back to Athens, then you make tourism."

"No, then we go home." His eyebrows shot up. "You come from England all the way to this little island, you stay three weeks, then you go straight home again!"

"Yes," she said. "We may stay in Athens for a day or two but that's all."

"But this is one of the lost islands," he said. "Nobody comes here."

"You came yourself," she pointed out.

"Ah, I bring my children. It is very good here for children."

"I think it will be very good for us too," Antonia said.

"Then you want rest, you want quiet. These you will find. But for three weeks . . . ! I know many people come to the hotel, but not to stay three weeks! All these you see today will be gone in a few days. There are no bus tours, nothing cultural. I think you will not stay three weeks. But anything you want to know while you are here, it will be my pleasure to advise you. My name is Mr. Apodiacos."

"Thank you, you're very kind," Antonia said.

"You must, for instance, go to Mr. Mobey's aquarium. It is very interesting. And you must always eat fish. The meat here is nothing, but the fish is excellent."

"We've just met Mr. Mobey," Antonia said, "but we don't know anything about his aquarium."

"Yes, it is his, I think so," Mr. Apodiacos said. "It was his father who built it in past times in the old windmill you see on the shore. This Mr. Mobey has improved it. He is a very rich man, I think. But he likes to live very simply here on this island. He also likes very much rest, very much quiet!"

He gave a hearty laugh. He seemed to find something highly ridiculous and perhaps not quite creditable in the idea of any foreigner wanting rest and quiet so badly that he would remain in one spot in Greece for more than two or three days.

The laugh made his paunch heave up and down. It already had a patch of sunburn on it, which was going to make it exceedingly painful for him to laugh when the skin started to blister, Antonia thought as she thanked him again and she and Tessa turned back toward the hotel.

They had a drink together on the terrace before dinner. The terrace faced the hill with the rocks at its summit. In the early southern twilight the whiteness of the houses built up the slopes became like a fleecy shawl wrapped about the hill's bowed old shoulders. The few lights shining here and there were like jewels caught in its folds. The sky changed from rose to lavender and the flowery scents in the air grew sweeter and stronger. Then a donkey brayed somewhere close at hand and another answered it, and then another, and presently the deepening shadows everywhere were filled with their evening hymn. It must be almost the mournfulest sound on earth, Antonia thought, and full of a quite preposterous pathos.

At another table on the terrace the young American was playing chess against himself, with a glass of tonic water at his elbow and his back turned to his two compatriots, who were drinking Scotch and reading paperback thrillers. A group of Greeks were drinking ouzo and chatting comfortably. It was all very peaceful except for a short time when a policeman, a burly man in a gray-green uniform with three white stripes on his cuff and most impractical-looking, pointed patent-leather shoes, strode in and started talking to Mrs. Marinatos, the manageress, a very portly little woman with abundant white hair, a guileless smile and watchful eyes.

All that he wanted was to look at the passports of the new arrivals, but the moment he appeared Mrs. Marinatos started to run up and down the entrance hall like a frantic bird trapped behind the mystery of a pane of glass and prepared to batter itself to death to escape from this incomprehensible menace. While she ran she talked faster and faster, drowning everything that the policeman said, and made Antonia remark to Tessa that modern Greek, when spoken with sufficient excitement, sounded exactly like the rattle of a typewriter.

"I wish I could talk it, all the same," Tessa said. "I'm beginning to feel dreadfully ashamed when they all talk such good English to me."

"I stopped feeling ashamed about that long ago," Antonia replied. "I just feel tremendously grateful."

They had dinner early and soon after it said goodnight to one another and Antonia went to her room.

Lying on her bed, she read for a while, but her thoughts wandered. She thought about the policeman, tried to recall his face, tried to imagine herself telling him that she had been followed here all the way from London by a man who believed that she was somebody else and quite possibly was intending to murder her. . . .

No, she would never be able to do that. The policeman had looked a level-headed sort of man, whom she would certainly trust to find her a furnished house for a holiday, but he would never be able to make head or tail of such a preposterous story. And it might have to be told through an interpreter, which would make it sound even worse. Yet she wouldn't be able to keep her fears bottled up indefinitely. She would have to talk to somebody sometime. Or run away.

Suddenly she longed to do that, to pack, to go home. But there was no ship until Monday.

She got up again restlessly. Opening the shutters, which had been closed earlier by the maid against the insects and the dangers of the night air, she went out onto her small balcony. The night was moonless, but a slight wind had risen and the foam of the waves as they broke made a glittering line of white along the edge of the sea's immense darkness. As she went out the sound of their breaking grew louder. So did a sound of voices below, voices that came from the direction of Tessa's balcony.

Because of the overhang of her own balcony, Antonia could not see Tessa herself, but only her shadow lying across the patch of light that fell from her window. She appeared to be leaning on the railing of her balcony and she was talking to the man in the checked shirt, who was standing on the path below it. The light that fell on his face marked it with sharp shadows, making triangular patches on his cheeks and a band like a narrow mask across his eyes, which gave him a dubious, harlequin's charm. Smiling up at Tessa, he reached for her hand.

Antonia retreated quickly into her room. She shut the doors and leaned against them. For a moment she could not get her breath.

# CHAPTER SIX

In the night the weather changed. The breeze shifted its direction and began to blow in powerful gusts. Wakened by the brightness of the dawn light, Antonia heard the shutters rattling against their fastenings and the waves crashing on the beach below. Hoping that the wind would have blown itself out by the time that she normally got up, she rolled over and went to sleep again.

But when she was later roused by the maid with her breakfast tray, the roar of the breakers was even louder and the sky was broken with hurrying clouds. It put her off any thought of swimming or of sunning herself on the beach. But she did not want to go looking for Tessa either to suggest a walk. She still needed a little time to get over the shock of what she had seen the evening before. So it was a relief presently to see that Tessa was busy playing a game on the sand with a large rubber ball and most of Mr. Apodiacos' daughters. Her hair was flying and she was looking wild and happy. Unpleasant suspicions apart, it seemed a good idea to leave her to it. Antonia went downstairs, went out into the battering wind and started to climb the hill.

She found, when she had gone only a little way, that when Mr. Apodiacos had spoken of the town as "upstairs," he had only been speaking literally, for after a quarter of a mile the road changed into a winding, stony staircase. At first the steps were wide and shallow and quite easy to climb, but soon they became much steeper and narrower, with older, more uneven paving, and Antonia began to pant as she toiled upward between the straight walls of the white boxlike houses.

As usual, there were flowers everywhere, orange trumpet-flowers, crimson dahlias, sunflowers, zinnias, roses. Here and there Antonia caught a glimpse through an open doorway of a shadowy room with carved wooden furniture and rows of burnished copper dishes hanging on the walls. Women and children went by with waterjugs on their shoulders. Most of the women smiled at her and murmured "*Kalimera*." The children, with laughter, called out, "Goodbye-ice-cream!"—a curious greeting, since they seemed neither to be soliciting donations of ice cream nor feeling any unfriendly wish to be rid of her.

Donkeys and mules, carrying loads of all sorts, ambled easily up and down the steps. One donkey that overtook her as she struggled upward had a pair of wooden boxes slung across its back with a goat reclining comfortably in each. Nothing can look more superior than a goat when it chooses, and these two, from their privileged position, leered down at her most impertinently as they passed.

The steps grew steeper still as they approached the base of the rocks. The look of them began to intimidate her as she thought that, if she went up them, she would have to come down again. Coming down was always the worst part, the hardest on inefficient feet. Standing still, she looked around her.

She was among the shops of the town. Some of them were splendid with glowing heaps of fresh fruit and vegetables, some were full of dusty ironmongery and unusable-looking plastic oddments, one had the carcass of a sheep hanging from a hook outside the door, from which the head could only just have been severed, for the blood was still dripping from the neck, making a puddle on the stones around which the flies were hungrily buzzing. There were several small cafés with tables set outside them under awnings. A great oleander grew at the side of the street, smothered in pink blossom.

At a table in front of one of the cafés a man was sitting alone. As Antonia paused, he raised his head and gave her a hard stare. For a moment she stood there helplessly, not knowing what to do next, then all of a sudden she found that there was no problem. Going straight toward him, she drew a chair up to his table and sat down.

"Dr. Livingstone, I presume," she said.

Startled, he began to get to his feet, then sank down again. A slight blush spread over his sallow face.

"As a matter of fact, my name *is* Stanley," he said. "Stanley Smith."

"Well, that's better than John Smith," she said. "I congratulate you on your imaginativeness, Mr. Smith."

"Thank you." He gave her a bewildered smile, as if to humor a harmless eccentric.

"Now don't you think it's time we had a talk?" she said.

"Glad to," he said. "Is it about anything special?"

His voice was as Tessa had described it, a curiously dramatic one, much fuller and deeper than Antonia had expected would issue from his rather scraggy throat.

"First I want you to tell me who you think I am," she said.

"Oh, that's easy. I think you're Mrs. Winfield," he answered agreeably, keeping up the act of politely indulging her craziness. "And I think you're the aunt of that girl . . ." He stopped, as if he had just seen light. "But it's quite all right, Mrs. Winfield, I know she's married and all that. A pity from my point of view. She's the only attractive girl in the place. But she's toting around a very big sign saying, 'Keep off the grass!' . . ." He stopped again. A waiter had just strolled out from the café and come to their table for their orders.

Antonia asked him for lemonade. Her companion asked for beer. The waiter went indoors again and set a jukebox going for their benefit. Its music started up a war with the music from a small transistor on a neighboring table, over which two young men sat in dreaming silence with thimble-sized cups of coffee before them, but the new noise did not seem to distract them. They were both in rough working clothes, with wide-brimmed straw hats pushed to the backs of their heads and sandals made from strips of old motor tire, an economical sort of footgear that seemed very popular on the island. Both had light brown curly hair. There were not many dark-haired people here, Antonia had noticed. Stanley Smith was much darker than most of them.

The waiter brought the lemonade and the beer and a dish of small green pears and Stanley Smith brought a handful of change out of his pocket and held it out. The waiter picked out a few coins and, when Stanley Smith added another, touched his heart lightly in a graceful gesture of thanks.

As he left them, Antonia asked, "Do you always hold

your money out like that and let them help themselves?"

"Why not?" he said. "It's the easiest thing to do and it's all right, you don't get gypped."

"But you know Greece, don't you?" she said. "I'd have thought you could cope with the money."

"Never been here before," he answered.

"But I've heard you speaking Greek."

"Oh, that. Yes, I do a bit. I lived in Egypt when I was a kid—my father was in the army—and you pick up a bit of most languages there."

"Is that why you were given the job of following me here?"

He looked at her blankly. It was not a very convincing blankness, because there was too much intelligence in his sharp dark eyes.

"I beg your pardon," he said. "Did you say I've been following you?"

"Ever since last Tuesday morning, or even earlier, but that's when I noticed it first. At the bus stop on Haverstock Hill."

He shook his head. "I don't think I've been up that way for years, Mrs. Winfield."

"Look, Mr. Smith," she said, "we both know you've been following me since last Tuesday, so pretending to me that you haven't isn't going to get us anywhere. The urgent thing just now, probably for you as well as for me, is for you to realize you've been following the wrong woman. If it's a Mrs. Winfield you're supposed to be following, you've got the wrong Mrs. Winfield."

"I'm sorry, I don't get this thing about following you," he said. "So far as I know, I saw you for the first time on the boat coming here yesterday. Are you sure you aren't mixing me up with some other chap?"

"Please," she said impatiently, "that's only wasting our time."

"Well, if you really think I've been following you," he said, "why haven't you complained? That's what I'd do in your place."

"I'm complaining now," she said. "I'm complaining very bitterly."

"I mean, to the police or someone."

"You know why I haven't," she said. "It's too fantastic for anyone to believe."

He gave a little grin. "Perhaps it is. But there's a policeman just over there." He nodded toward a group of men playing tricktrack in the café across the street. "If you're so worried, why not go and tell him your troubles? He's the *Astynomos*, the police chief of this island, I've been told. It's true he probably saw you come and join me of your own accord, which is a thing women don't much do in cafés in Greece, so it won't have passed unnoticed. But I'll promise not to argue. I'll sit quietly and let you do all the talking."

Antonia looked at the group of men. She realized that one of them was the man who had come to the hotel to inspect the passports of the new arrivals. He was not in uniform now, but in gray trousers and an open-necked shirt, with his head bare.

"That's a third of the police force of the island off duty," she remarked. "I wonder if there's never any crime on Saturdays."

"Probably there isn't much crime here on any day of the week," Stanley Smith said. "Go on, Mrs. Winfield, or you'll lose your chance."

For the *Astynomos* had just stood up. The game appeared to be finished. He took leave of the others and walked off down the hill, pausing to chat for a moment with a man who was driving a donkey up it, a lean old man with rugged features baked hard and dry by the sun, huge, baggy blue trousers, leggings and the usual sandals cut from motor tires. The donkey was carrying two flat wooden boxes filled with fish. As the man and donkey came on, word of their arrival went around as if by magic, doors opened and women came running out with baskets or dishes, to trail them up the hill to a spot where the fishmonger's wife was setting up a pair of scales and preparing to sell the new consignment.

"Thank you," Antonia said, "but when I go to the police, it's going to be in my own time. All I want at the moment is to make you understand that you've got hold of the wrong Mrs. Winfield. What you want with the other one I don't know, but you're only losing your time, trailing after me, and you're ruining my holiday while you're about it."

"I'm sorry about that," he said. "Awfully sorry. Only I don't know just what I can do about it, do you?"

"You could try to take in what I'm telling you, *that I'm not this other woman!*"

"There is no other woman."

He said it flatly, without emphasis, yet a feeling of cold swept through her, as if the wind had suddenly found its way up the narrow street.

"There must be," she said. "If you'd tell me about her—tell me what she's like—I'm sure I could persuade you you've made a mistake."

"Look, Mrs. Winfield," he said, "why don't you just stop worrying? Or if you must go on worrying about something, why not worry about someone else for a change? It might be better worth your while."

"I don't want to worry about anything!" she said indignantly. "I only want to be left alone to enjoy my stay here."

"All right then, why not decide it was two other people all the time?" he said. "Some other chap was following some other woman."

The policeman had reappeared and was coming up the hill again. He had a little boy by the hand and was carrying a basket and he too joined the crowd following the donkey with the load of fish. A charming sight, Antonia thought. The policeman looked a nice man, a kind, domesticated man and devoted to his little son. But not a man, somehow, to whom she could tell her particular story.

"You know, I believe this is the most extraordinary situation I've ever been in in my life," she said. "It's like being in a dream."

"That's what people come to this sort of place for, isn't it?" Stanley Smith said. "To live in a sort of dream for a little while."

"Which seems to have the knack of turning into a nightmare."

"Oh yes, if you look around you I expect you'll find as many nightmares going on here as anywhere else," he agreed pleasantly. "People have pretty much the same things to be afraid of everywhere. There's always disease, madness, poverty, failure, death. . . ." He broke off as if he had just realized that he was speaking words that had not been written into his script. Repeating vaguely, "Look around you," he made a gesture with one of his slender hands which took in the two men sitting in a trance of pleasure over their transistor, and a priest with his beard and his little bun of hair under his high black hat, sitting at a table across the street, reading a newspaper and drinking ouzo, and a woman, all in the customary black of the elderly, with her face muffled in her black headcloth, going by with a surprisingly sprightly walk, using a long bamboo cane to support her, and the middle-aged American couple from the hotel, who were coming panting up the hill.

They greeted Antonia and Stanley Smith with cries of, "Hello there!" The man went on, "This seems like a good spot you've found. Mrs. Ball and I have spent the morning looking for a place to get out of the wind. Nobody ever told us about this wind before. I'm coming to believe it blows round and round this island in both directions at the same time. It's too cold on the beach for anyone but your niece, Mrs. Winfield, and that young compatriot of ours. They're swimming and in between playing chess. I'd have thought a boy and girl like that could find something better to do than play chess, but from the way they look when they're playing you can see they hardly know what's going on around them."

Antonia remembered that Roger had taught Tessa the game when she was a child.

"Yes, my niece has always been very fond of it," she said. "She's quite a good player, I believe."

"In my opinion there's something the matter with that boy," Mrs. Ball said. "Any time we speak to him he looks like we were insulting him. I don't know what we've done to offend him. I guess maybe he has a Problem and needs Help." She gave the two words rather sinister capital letters.

"It can't be much of a problem if he can spend his vacation wandering around Greece," her husband said. "I had to spend mine waiting tables. This is the first time Mrs. Ball and I have been back to the Old Country. We live in New Jersey, but we're both of Greek descent. My father's name was Balalas but I guess he found Ball a lot easier to spell!"

"A game like chess," said Mrs. Ball, broodingly pursuing her own line of thought, "it isn't a constructive activity for a boy his age. It's an escape, it's a flight from reality. It's a way of cutting yourself off from other people. I tell you, if I was that boy's mother, I'd really worry about him."

"You make me feel perhaps I'd better go and rescue Tessa from his clutches," Antonia said. She felt that this conversation, breaking straight into the one that she had been having with Stanley Smith, might drive her right over the edge into lunacy. As she stood up she and the Balls all said that it was nice to have met one another and she started down the hill. Rather to her surprise, Stanley Smith went with her and she found that, when the rough steps tilted more steeply than usual, it was useful to have his arm to hold. But she had lost the will to go on trying to make him understand her or to find out any more about him. When they spoke, it was only of the things and the people they passed and the wind that sprang at them as soon as they left the shelter of the houses.

When they reached the hotel the manageress met Antonia with the message that Mrs. Foley and Mr. Lambrick, the young American, had taken a picnic lunch with them and gone walking.

Antonia on the whole was cheered by the news. She did not mind whose company Tessa sought so long as it was not Stanley Smith's.

He and she went to their separate tables in the dining room and ate a lunch of moussaka and huge chunks of watermelon, and afterward Antonia went to her room and lay down, expecting to fall asleep, as she was inclined to after a large lunch, but for once her mind was restlessly active. A plan of sorts was beginning to form in it, perhaps not a very wonderful plan, but to have a plan of any kind felt better than nothing. . . .

Meanwhile, there was the rest of the day to fill in.

The wind had subsided a little and the fierce gray-green of the sea had changed back to blue, but it was still too rough for Antonia's idea of a pleasant bathe. Getting up, she changed out of the blouse and skirt that she had put on that morning into her new dress, which still had a good effect on her morale, and set out to visit Mr. Mobey's aquarium.

To begin with she walked along the shore. But plowing through the soft sand was tiring, and after she had gone a little way she left the beach, climbed the slope between two cottages, skirted a field of tomatoes behind them and went on along a track that led through fields of maize and bearded wheat toward the old windmill on the point.

Because it was afternoon hardly a soul was stirring. On the beach she had seen no one but a ragged boy sound asleep in the lee of a boat, and a woman in black, like the one whom she had seen in the town that morning, or perhaps the very same one, resting on a rock. As Antonia went by, the woman got up and began to plod slowly along the slope, leaning on her bamboo cane. Poor old thing, Antonia thought. With her muffled face and her clumsy draperies sweeping the ground, she was as depressing a sight as the half-clad sleeping boy was beautiful.

Yet it turned out that the old woman, when she chose, was a pretty fast walker. She left the beach at the same spot as Antonia and soon began to catch up with her. Presently, when Antonia glanced behind her, she wondered why she had taken for granted that the woman was old. You couldn't tell much about her under all that bedraggled black, but there was something about her long, gliding stride that suggested youth.

But the young women of the island didn't dress like that. They wore ordinary modern cotton dresses, high heels and make-up. And even the old women, the bent and toothless ones, the ones who sat in doorways with spindles whirring in their arthritic fingers, didn't cover their faces. Not on this island. It was one of the pleasant things about the place. The Moslems had not left that particular blight behind them here, as in many other parts of Greece.

The woman came on quickly until she was about ten paces behind Antonia. But when Antonia walked slower and moved to the side of the path so that she could pass, the other woman only walked slower too. Then, when Antonia started to hurry, the other woman hurried.

Antonia walked on with growing uneasiness. She knew that the sensible thing to do was to stand still and ask the woman what she wanted. She might simply be trying to pluck up her courage to beg, although so far Antonia had seen no beggars here, any more than she had seen veiled faces. Or perhaps the poor woman was not quite right in the head and was following her only out of a primitive sort of curiosity. But during the last few days a panicky horror of being followed had been born in Antonia, and she felt that if she did not take great care she might lose her head and do something ridiculous, like starting to run or to scream for help. And with those soft footsteps in the dust pounding closer and closer to her, it was useless to pretend that she hadn't noticed the woman.

Abruptly she stood still and turned.

It took the woman in black by surprise. For an instant she stood still too. Then she started to come on again. But at just that moment a donkey with a great load of lucerne on its back emerged onto the path between them from behind some bushy pomegranates and began to amble in the direction of the windmill.

The donkey was followed by another, and this by a mule, and this by an old man with a rake over his shoulder, yawning and rubbing the afternoon sleep from his eyes. The island was beginning to wake up again.

Antonia walked on quickly, keeping ahead of the donkeys. The woman in black took a few steps after them, then turned and started to walk slowly back the way that she had come.

When Antonia reached the windmill she found a notice board on the door on which it was stated in Greek, English, French and German that the museum was closed every afternoon until four-thirty.

It was past four-thirty now, but the door was still shut. However, a man who was working on some net spread out on the sand nearby saw Antonia, called out to her and came trotting over to her. He flung open the door, which was not locked, inviting her with a gesture to enter, started switching on lights and demanded three drachmas.

The lights illuminated a circular chamber with white walls which were lined with rather dusty-looking glass cabinets, full of seaweeds, sea shells, stuffed fish of every size from sharks to minnows, and strange varieties of fishing tackle. Antonia did not think it looked very interesting. But wanting to have her three drachmas worth, she was starting to look around when she found the man ushering her with more inviting gestures to a door in the wall.

"Down!" he cried enthusiastically. "Down, down!"

She took a cautious look through the doorway.

A narrow spiral staircase descended between walls of white glazed tiles.

She hesitated, but the man pressed more light switches and smilingly repeated, "Down!"

She grasped the handrail and started downward. The man did not follow her but went to lounge at the open door.

As she went round and round the steep spiral, going deeper, a powerful smell rose to meet her, which was like the concentration of all sea smells. There was sheer wetness and saltiness in it, and fishiness and rottenness. This must be how it smelled, she thought, at the bottom of the sea. In spite of the white tiles and the electric light, it made her think of wrecks and dead men's bones and waving forests of dark weed.

At the foot of the stairs the white tiles stopped. A low archway of rough stone faced her. Beyond the arch, a passage curved away to right and left into a greenish twilight. The sea smell grew even stronger.

She had to fight off a feeling of claustrophobia before she could go on. But taking a deep breath and holding it, just as if she had been about to submerge herself in the sea, she stepped through the archway.

At the next moment she let the breath out with an exclamation of pleasure. Along each side of the dim passage, comfortably at eye level, fish tanks had been set in the roughly hewn walls. The tanks were softly lit from within and air bubbles rose gently through the water from hidden pipes and delicate curtains of colored weed stirred gently as all kinds of strange sea creatures moved among them. There were small fish with long, weaving fins tinted like flowers. There were lean and darting fish, moving like swift knives through the water. There were long dark creatures that lay in coils at the bottom of their tank and, when they stirred a little, seemed to express a limitless menace. There was an octopus which fixed Antonia with a glare of pure hatred from a huge, furious eye, then spread lacy white skirts and performed a dance of wild grace for her benefit.

Entranced, she went on from tank to tank. In one of them, bigger than the rest, several turtles swam on and on in slow, deliberate figures of eight. In spite of their thick bodies and the shells on their backs, there was nothing heavy or clumsy about them. They were beautifully balanced with each movement of a stubby flipper, a wonder of economy and strength. Antonia stood still for several minutes watching their dignified reel, and was so absorbed in it that it was far too late for her to do anything to protect herself when out of the corner of her eye she noticed a movement in the shadows.

It was too late to run then, to look around for something to use as a weapon. She did not even scream until it was all over and the black figure with the veiled face and the bamboo cane grasped like a spear had leapt at her, snatched the belt of gold coins from around her waist and fled.

# CHAPTER SEVEN

The sound of heavy footsteps pounding down the stairs and along the passage were at first a new terror from which she must somehow fly. But then a man's voice called out and the man who had let her into the museum appeared around the curve of the passage.

He exclaimed with relief when he saw her. She realized then that she must have screamed most horribly after the creature in black had gone, for the man seemed to have been expecting to find that murder or rape had been done. Grasping her arm to support her, he started talking swiftly, gesturing at the tank where the turtles swam tranquilly on and on. Though he spoke in Greek, Antonia guessed that he was telling her that all the monsters were safe behind glass, that they could not harm her. Nodding, thanking him, glad of his flood of human speech, even if it was not to the point, and intensely grateful to him for his human concern after the reptilian silence, she let him lead her up into the daylight.

He took her straight to the open door of the mill. It felt wonderful to have the sky over her head again, to breathe air cleansed by sun and wind and free of the dank sub-marine taint. The man went on talking to her. He was ask-ing her, she supposed, what had happened to frighten her. She tried to remember the words for "a woman in black." *Mavro* was black, wasn't it? She began, "*Mavro* . . ." then gave it up and pointed to her waist, from which the belt had gone.

Naturally he took it as a way of saying that she felt pain there. Making soothing gestures and persuading her to sit down on the sand, he set off at a jog trot toward the nearest cottage.

Before he was halfway there he was intercepted by a stout figure in swimming trunks, a broad-brimmed straw hat and sunglasses. Pouring out his story, the man pointed to where he had left Antonia. Mr. Apodiacos came hurry-ing up to her.

"Mrs. Winfield!" he cried. "The man tells me you are ill. Can I help you? You should not stay here in the sun. Can you walk a little? Let us go back into the museum where you can rest while we send him to telephone for a doctor."

She had stood up again as soon as the man had left her and had been looking around her. She could see for a long way along the curving shore and along the path through the fields. A few men and women were working there. A boy was driving a donkey along the beach, hitting it at every few steps for no particular reason except that it was his boyish nature to do so. There were two or three intrepid bathers in the choppy sea. She recognized the two Germans among them. But she could not see any woman in black.

"No, thank you, it's good of you, but I'm not ill at all," she replied. "It's just that—well, an extraordinary thing happened and I got frightened."

"Ah, I see, I see. You suffer with claustrophobia. I too," Mr. Apodiacos said. "It is like being in a prison in a small cell and one will never get out and the walls will soon close in on one and crush one. Is that it? But the man said you were in great pain and you look very pale. I think we should send for a doctor."

"No, truly I'm not in any pain," she said. "If I want anyone, it's a policeman. I've just had something stolen from me."

"Stolen? Here?"

"Yes."

"But who by, Mrs. Winfield? Who was there? Not this man. I assure you, he is a very good, honest man."

"Yes, he was very kind. No, it was a woman, a small woman all in black."

Mr. Apodiacos gave her a long look which his sun glasses made inscrutable and disturbing.

"What did she steal?" he asked. "Your handbag? No, you have it. Something from your handbag, then? Some money?"

"No, just the belt I was wearing," Antonia said.

"A *belt?*"

"I know it sounds absurd," she said. "It wasn't of any value. At least, I don't think it was. It really belongs to my niece. But the woman followed me a long way to get it."

"This woman in black?"

"Yes, with her face covered. I saw her first on the beach quite near the hotel and she followed me all the way here. At one point I thought she'd turned back and gone the other way, but when I was down in the aquarium she suddenly appeared again and snatched my belt and ran off. She didn't try to hurt me, but I lost my head and started screaming. It was just the shock of it and the queer light and all those creatures swimming and swimming . . ."

Mr. Apodiacos had listened with a frown of intense concentration. She was afraid that perhaps she had spoken too rapidly for him. He turned to the other man and spoke to him in Greek. The man shook his head and gestured at his fishing nets. Mr. Apodiacos pressed his questions. The man answered at some length. Mr. Apodiacos fingered his chin doubtfully. Frowning still, he looked back at Antonia.

"He says he saw no woman, Mrs. Winfield. He saw no one but you. But he admits he was mending his nets and not paying attention as he should."

"But didn't you see her yourself, Mr. Apodiacos?" Antonia asked. "You were here on the beach. Didn't you see her come out?"

"I see no one such as you describe," he said. "But I am not paying attention either. I am looking for seashells and pretty stones for my daughters. Now I tell you what we do. We call on Mr. Mobey. That is his house there. We go to him and ask him if he sees this woman."

Antonia felt certain that Mr. Mobey would not have seen her. She had begun to feel a superstitious certainty that it would turn out that no one had seen her.

Mr. Apodiacos saw her hesitating and said, "Even if he saw nothing, it does no harm to ask and it is good he knows what happens in his aquarium. He would wish it."

"Very well," Antonia said and turned obediently toward the nearest of the white cottages.

Mr. Mobey saw them coming from his veranda and hurried out to meet them. The wind lifted his neat white hair above his head in a shining cockscomb, his pink cheeks glowed.

"Just what I was wishing!" he exclaimed. "I was longing for someone to drop in. A day of this wind and for some reason I always find myself pining for company, instead of being placidly satisfied with my own. I think perhaps it's because the wind itself has a kind of personality, a very intrusive kind of personality, which destroys the sense of solitude and yet isn't in the least companionable or friendly. I've yet to meet a really friendly wind, I believe. Even a gentle breeze is never entirely to be trusted, any more than those friends one has who can sit drinking with one so pleasantly and then, on half a glass too much, suddenly start smashing the furniture."

"Mr. Mobey!" Mr. Apodiacos interrupted. "Mr. Mobey! Please, we have come to tell you a most shocking thing."

He plunged quickly into Antonia's story.

When it came to an end, Mr. Mobey gave Antonia a look of great concern.

"Mrs. Winfield, I'm appalled that you should have had such a horrid experience," he said. "Down in that fishy cavern too. It must have been quite terrifying. I can only suggest, by way of cheer, that it would have been even worse if the thief had been a six-foot man instead of a small woman."

They had reached the veranda. Over their heads a bamboo canopy screeched and rattled in the gusts and there was a gritty feeling of blown sand in the air.

"We'll sit indoors, don't you think?" Mr. Mobey went on. "But I must ask you to ignore a bachelor's untidiness. An excellent woman cleans for me, but I don't allow her to move a single scrap of paper, or any other object, for that matter, without express permission. Now what will you have to drink, Mrs. Winfield? Whisky? Brandy?"

Mr. Apodiacos said, "Mrs. Winfield should drink ouzo. Nothing opens the appetite and makes gay so quickly."

"True, true," Mr. Mobey said, "but perhaps at the moment Mrs. Winfield doesn't aspire to becoming very gay. A somewhat grave atmosphere of rational clear-headedness may be more appropriate. Myself, I recommend brandy for someone who's been seeing things down among the fish."

He ushered them into the house. Waving them to chairs, he disappeared into another room, from which he reappeared in a moment with a tray and glasses.

The untidiness of which he had spoken consisted only of a few books and papers strewn about the room. Otherwise it was furnished in much the same way as the rooms that Antonia had seen through open doors on her way up the hill. The walls were washed a pale blue. There was a low wooden settle, covered with a fine piece of peasant embroidery. There were some carved wooden chairs, a table, an old iron lamp hanging from a hook in the ceiling and two rows of shining copper dishes on one wall. Only a crowded bookcase, a record player and an Anglepoise lamp beside the one large, comfortable armchair made the room different from all those other rooms.

Mr. Mobey poured out brandy for Antonia and himself and ouzo for Mr. Apodiacos.

"And now please tell me again just what happened, Mrs. Winfield," he said as he sat down with them. "This little woman snatched your belt, you say—that very charming belt I saw you wearing yesterday?"

"Yes, that was all," Antonia said.

"And she followed you for some distance, presumably intending to steal it?"

"Yes, all the way from the hotel."

"Poor thing, poor thing," Mr. Mobey said. "A poor, very ignorant woman who imagined the coins were real ones, don't you think that's the explanation? Or perhaps she's a bit deranged, a bit round the bend, and the glitter of the thing caught her eye. In any case, very sad and very horrid for you. I hope you're beginning to feel better. I'm always inclined to get the jitters down there myself. It's quite the most frightening place I know."

"Mr. Mobey," Antonia said, the brandy steadying her, "I did really see her, you know. She did really snatch my belt. I mention that because of what you said just now about seeing things down in that fishy cavern. I mean, I *wasn't* just seeing things."

"But of course, of course!" He looked distressed. "I beg your pardon if I seemed to imply . . . No, no, I was just trying to express my sympathy. A fright's always so much worse in a frightening place." He turned to Mr. Apodiacos. "You were near, Mr. Apodiacos? You saw her too?"

"That is what I was going to ask you," Mr. Apodiacos said. "Did you see her, Mr. Mobey? Unfortunately I saw nothing. I was not looking in the direction of the windmill. Nor was your man, who should have been looking after it."

"Wasn't he, indeed? He'll hear from me, then. But probably he didn't think we could possibly have two customers in one afternoon. And nothing of the sort has ever happened here before. Nor anywhere else on the island, that I ever heard of. They're very quiet, law-abiding people."

"Yes, if there is any trouble, it is always with foreigners," Mr. Apodiacos said. Then, realizing to whom he had said it, he amended, "Not foreigners like you and Mr. Mobey, Mrs. Winfield. Other Greeks. That is what I mean. Always other Greeks, not the people of this island. Even in the war, when they only had the Italians here, there was no trouble. They are not warlike people, the Italians. The Germans only let them stay where they knew there would be no trouble. Not in Crete, for instance. Oh, no! In Crete every man is a hero. If he doesn't carry a gun, he thinks he is a woman. But here they are friends with everybody. Civilization has not touched them yet."

"That reminds me," Antonia said, "there are two Germans staying at the hotel, who were swimming near the windmill when I came out. Perhaps they saw the woman. I understand you didn't, Mr. Mobey?"

"No, I didn't, I'm afraid," he said. "I was probably sound asleep when she went by. But now we come to the question, what do you wish to do about it? Shall we call the police?"

"Oh yes," Mr. Apodiacos said decidedly. "Certainly we must do so. We can't have our visitors robbed."

"I think the same myself," Mr. Mobey said. "I don't like the idea of mysterious goings-on in my museum and should prefer to have them investigated. But clearly it's for Mrs. Winfield to decide. She may feel that as the belt itself wasn't of any great value and that as interviews with the police have a way of upsetting the peace and quiet one looks for on a holiday, she'd prefer to do nothing."

"Peace and quiet, peace and quiet!" Mr. Apodiacos gave a shout of laughter. "I find it so funny you come to Greece for peace and quiet. No, Mrs. Winfield, when you come to Greece, you should come to live dangerously. Think of our history. Think of all you know about us. Listen, I tell you something. Do you know why our shipbuilders now in Greece are so successful? It is because they are not afraid to live dangerously. In Britain you are afraid of debt, you are afraid of risks. But here a man wants to build ships, he goes to the bank, he says, 'I want to build ships but I have no money, will you lend me some, please?' The bank says, 'Gladly!' The man says, 'I don't pay you back, you take my ships, you take all.' You see, he is not afraid to live dangerously and so he becomes very, very rich."

"I've never yet heard a bank say, 'Gladly!'" Antonia said. "I didn't know they could. Apart from that . . ." She turned to look consideringly at Mr. Mobey. "I think you're trying tactfully to give me a way out, in case, when it comes to the point, I decide I don't really want to tell the police a lot of stuff and nonsense about being followed by someone who never existed. But as I said before, she does exist, she did follow me, she did steal my belt."

"Please, please, Mrs. Winfield!" Mr. Mobey laid his hand on hers. "I don't know what I've done to make you so suspicious of me. I assure you, I haven't doubted your story for one moment. Come now, have a little more brandy."

"Of course, if we send for the police, it'll spoil the poor man's day off," she went on. "And I suppose the belt itself doesn't matter much, though it isn't mine, so I don't really know. And the woman, as you say, is probably just some poor crazy old soul. . . ." She paused. Both men were watching her intently and suddenly it seemed to her that there was something strange in that intentness. The mild gaze of Mr. Mobey's blue eyes and the dark stare of Mr. Apodiacos' sunglasses were both just too steady. Why should it matter to either of them whether or not she called the police?

Picking her words with care, she went on, "But she wasn't old, I'm certain of that from the way she moved. Her hands weren't old, or her eyes. I had a glimpse of them over the black scarf-thing she wore over her face. They were very big and dark. Perhaps they were mad, I don't know, but they weren't old. And the local women don't cover their faces like that, do they? So I think, whoever she was, she's deliberately disguised herself to follow me."

"To steal a belt that was of no value?" Mr. Apodiacos said, putting his head on one side.

"I can't tell you. In any case, I think it would be an excellent thing to call the police. I'll be very glad to tell them everything."

"Good," Mr. Mobey said. "I'm sure it's the proper thing to do."

He got up and went to the telephone.

While they waited for the police to arrive, he told Antonia some of the history of his aquarium. His father had been a keen amateur naturalist who had fallen in love with the island, had settled there and started his collection, housing it in the old mill. But it was his son who had seen the possibilities of the stone foundations and had put in lighting and fish tanks. Meanwhile his mother had always preferred Paris to any other spot on earth, and Mr. Mobey had spent most of his youth traveling backward and forward between France and Greece, except for an abominably uncomfortable period spent at a public school in England.

"Altogether a perfect recipe for turning out a totally useless individual," he said with a pleased smile, "particularly since I was aware from the start that I was unlikely ever to be under any compulsion to earn a living. But luckily, as I think, I inherited many of both my parents' tastes, so I've found the collection here a great source of interest, without its ever gaining an obsessional hold on my mind. Paris, Rome, London, always reclaim me sooner or later. And while I'm here my fish have the immense charm of helping me to make new friends. Such delightful people come to my door with their questions."

His bland voice helped his brandy to calm Antonia's nerves. By the time that the *Astynomos,* back in his gray-green uniform, arrived, she was ready to tell her story composedly and to take for granted, as she normally did, that what she said would be believed.

The *Astynomos,* with Mr. Apodiacos and Mr. Mobey acting as interpreters, held out very good hopes that the woman would be traced almost immediately.

"Everything is known here," the policeman said. "Everything is observed and remembered. If she is a stranger here, that will have been noted by fifty people. If she lives here—but I feel sure myself she is a stranger—her actions will have attracted attention. I have no doubt at all I shall be able to return the lady's lost property to her tomorrow."

He departed briskly.

A few minutes later Antonia got up to go, Mr. Apodiacos leaving with her and walking back to the hotel with her.

As they strolled along, he remarked, "I don't think Mr. Mobey has any need of his fish to help him make friends. I think he is a man who makes friends everywhere. He has a great interest in all people he meets. I have the same temperament. I like very much to converse with strangers and learn what I can of their lives."

"Me too," Antonia replied absently, thinking that she would have to tell Tessa about the loss of the belt and that perhaps it would make her unhappy.

"Today I learn more than I expect," Mr. Apodiacos went on in a curiously insinuating tone, as if he were leading up to a question of some importance. "The whole affair is very strange. There are many things about it I do not understand. That belt, for instance, I am just wondering if it is true that it is not valuable."

"I think it's true," Antonia said. "Mr. Mobey thought so, didn't he?"

"But you do not know? Of your own knowledge, you do not know?"

"Not really."

"Well, you must not let it spoil your holiday. Remember what I say to you, Mrs. Winfield. Forget this peace and quiet you look for. It is no good to anybody. Enjoy what comes. Live dangerously."

"I don't seem to have much choice, do I?" she said. "But I'm afraid it's too much to expect me to enjoy it. I'm not that sort of person."

"Aren't you, Mrs. Winfield? Are you sure you are not?"

There was a note of challenge in his voice which made her look at him in surprise. Why hadn't it struck her before, she wondered, that there was something not exactly kind or gentle about his soft-lipped, genially smiling mouth? Perhaps she had never really looked at it. The sunglasses and the expanse of plump nakedness above his belt, with the spreading patch of sunburn that was just beginning to come up in blisters, had always distracted her.

On an impulse, she said, "Mr. Apodiacos, you did see that woman, didn't you?"

"You think so?" he said, still smiling. "Why?"

"There aren't any trees or bushes near the mill, or walls, or anything to hide behind. If you didn't see her leave the mill, at least you must have seen her walk up to it. Why didn't you tell the police you had?"

They had reached the entrance of the hotel.

"I think you do not tell them everything yourself, Mrs. Winfield?" he said as they stood still there. "And I think you do not speak Greek, so how do you know what I tell them?"

He gave a jolly laugh and walked off.

Antonia stood frowning after him, half-inclined to pursue him to make him explain what he meant, but then she went into the hotel.

She went to Tessa's room. Tessa had returned from her walk with the American, had been having a shower, from which she had just emerged, and was walking about the room in her dressing gown, brushing her hair.

As soon as she saw Antonia, she began, "You didn't mind my going off for the day, did you? I thought you'd like to be left in peace. Dave Lambrick and I have taken a long walk into the hills. It's quite different from anything I expected. I thought everything would be rather burnt up and colorless at this time of year, but there are huge banks of oleanders all over the place, and masses of a shrub with great purple spikes on it—I don't know what it's called, but Dave says it's what the Spartans used to birch their boys with—horrid Spartans! Dave's terrifically well-informed. He's over at Oxford for a year with a grant of some sort, and he's had several poems published already, and he's very sweet too. But I was telling you about that shrub. It's a glorious sight, because it gets completely covered with clouds and clouds of tortoiseshell butterflies. . . . Antonia, please, what's the matter?" It had just dawned on Tessa that something was wrong. The elation faded from her voice. "You aren't annoyed with me for going off, are you? It's been such a marvelous day. Haven't you had a nice day too?"

"I'll tell you what sort of a day I've had," Antonia said, dropping onto the edge of Tessa's bed and kicking off her sandals. "First I had a long talk with Stanley Smith. You've had more than one yourself, I believe, so I needn't tell you much about it. It got us precisely nowhere. Then I was followed along the beach by a little woman in black, who pounced on me suddenly when I was in Mr. Mobey's aquarium and stole the belt you lent me. Then I had a drink with Mr. Mobey and Mr. Apodiacos, the police came and I told them what had happened. And then Mr. Apodiacos walked back with me and advised me to live dangerously. That's been my nice quiet day."

All the cheerfulness had drained out of Tessa's face. "A woman in black who stole that belt . . . ?"

"Darling, I'm so sorry about it," Antonia said, reaching for her hand. "That the belt's gone I mean. But I never

dreamt that was what she was after. The police think
they'll get it back, and so they may, I suppose, if they're
right that she's just a poor insane creature who thought
the coins were real money. They'll trace her at once and
they'll find out what she's done with the thing and you'll
have it back quite quickly."

Tessa gave a shake of her head. "The belt doesn't matter. If it's gone, it's gone. But I don't understand what
happened. It sounds awful. Do tell it again properly."

Antonia once more described the day's events, this time
in detail.

At the end, Tessa said, "Well, I should think the police
are right, the woman's insane. There isn't any other possible explanation. It must have been horrible for you, but
there isn't anything to worry about."

"You think not?" Antonia said with an edge on her voice.

"Of course not."

"All the same, we're leaving this place on Monday."

She saw the sudden dismay in Tessa's eyes. Then she
turned away. "Why?" she asked in a subdued voice.

"It's a plan I thought up this afternoon. And I don't
want you to tell anyone at all about it. Not your friend
Dave Lambrick or anyone."

"Dave isn't any special friend of mine. I just like him."

"All right. Now listen. On Monday we'll take the ship
back to the mainland and find rooms somewhere for a few
days. My belief is that Stanley Smith will turn up there
immediately. However, if he doesn't, I promise I'll agree
I've been wrong about him and that the way I've kept
running into him has been just a vast coincidence, and
we'll come back here and finish our holiday peacefully.
But *if* he comes after us, you'll admit he's been following
me and we'll go to the police together and complain. *Together*, that's the point. Because they just might take it

seriously if there were two of us. Or if you don't like the idea of that, we'll pack up and go home. . . . Oh God, I know it isn't a very good plan, Tessa, but it's the only one I can think of."

It was a moment before Tessa appeared to realize that she had finished. Then she gave a soft sigh and started brushing her hair again.

"All right, we'll do that," she said.

"Well, can you suggest anything better?"

"No."

"Of course, if by any chance the belt was the thing they were after all along, they may fade out now. In that case, I suppose we can stay where we are."

"Antonia!" Tessa swung around. Her face looked cold and stern, which was one of her ways of looking frightened. "How could 'they' be after that belt? I mean, if 'they,' as you call them, are after anything. This man started following you about in London, so you say, before you even knew I'd be coming to see you that evening. You didn't even know the belt existed, so how could he? Or 'they'?"

"Yes," Antonia said. "Yes, of course, I'm sorry. I'm in a muddle." She slipped her feet back into her sandals and stood up. "I just thought that if by any chance it's really far more valuable than you think—"

"It isn't."

"But suppose it is."

"I was there when Alec bought it," Tessa said. "It cost fifty-two and sixpence in a junk shop in Chelsea. And Mr. Mobey said the coins were only imitations of some famous pieces, didn't he? Or do you think he's in the plot too? Do you think the woman in black was really hiding in his house all the time you were there?"

"Isn't that actually the simplest explanation?" Antonia

said. "Otherwise, how did she manage to vanish off the face of the earth so quickly? I'm now going upstairs to change and I'll meet you on the terrace for a drink in half an hour."

Tessa let her go in silence.

When they met on the terrace half an hour later the twilight was already blotting out the hills and the donkeys had begun their sad evening chanting. Blended with the piteous sound, a faint murmur of music moved mysteriously here and there, as if borne on the breeze. It came in fact from a transistor that was hung on a string around the neck of a boy who was watering the vegetable garden with a green plastic hose. The boy was as calm and as beautiful as ancient marble. The lights from the terrace turned the wavering arc of water from the hose into a stream of glittering crystal.

Antonia and Tessa sat down at a table and lit cigarettes. Antonia tried to will herself to relax, to let the charm of the evening work on her nerves. She had made her plan and Tessa had agreed to it. Nothing was to be gained by going on and on worrying.

Just then a voice spoke behind her, a voice almost as plaintive as the donkeys', but with a faint Glasgow accent.

"No, I've not been bored—don't dream of such a thing," it said. "No, I've not been impatient. If I've been bloody well browned off that's my own affair and the last thing I'd want is to have you worry about it. I love you and I want you to be happy and I quite understand you've got friends in all parts of the country, whose mothers are ill and whom you've got to go and visit. But when you go off by yourself for the whole day, why can't you tell me that's what you're going to do? That's all I'm asking—just to be told."

"So you know how long you have for getting drunk, maybe?" said a shrill girl's voice.

Remembering the couple whom she and Tessa had met in the bar of the hotel in Athens, Antonia looked over her shoulder.

There they were, the man sitting with his back to her, crouching despondently over the table, with one of his hands grasping a hand of his fiancée, the Greek girl with the remarkable eyes. It was only her eyes that Antonia took in of either of them now, for meeting them suddenly over the man's shoulder, which concealed the lower part of the girl's face, she was instantly filled with the blind certainty that they were the eyes that had met hers a few hours ago in the aquarium over the concealing folds of a black scarf.

# CHAPTER EIGHT

She said nothing about it. She had that much sense.

The girl had seen her turn, but gave no sign of recognition. She only began to chatter eagerly to the man, putting on a show of being wholly absorbed in him. After a little while they got up to go. Apparently they were not staying in the hotel but had only dropped in for a drink. Antonia watched them as they walked away into the dusk, the man with his arm around the girl's shoulders, the girl walking with jerky little steps and much swaying of the hips. It was not at all like the long, gliding stride of the woman in black. But the woman in black had not been wearing patent leather sandals with four-inch heels.

As they disappeared, Tessa remarked, "I wonder how they got here?"

Antonia lifted her eyebrows.

"Didn't you recognize them?" Tessa said. "They're those people you picked up in the bar in Athens."

"I know, but I didn't realize you'd recognize them too," Antonia said.

"I didn't want to encourage you to pick them up again," Tessa said with a smile.

"I'm too tired to want to talk to anyone, if I haven't got to."

"All the same, how did they get here?"

"Just as we did, I suppose."

"But they weren't on the ship with us yesterday, and I'm sure there hasn't been one in today."

"Perhaps they came by helicopter or submarine." Antonia was rather pleased with herself for being able to turn the question off with a joke. She elaborated it, "I expect they've a rival gang on the trail of our friend Stanley Smith. And here he comes," she added, seeing him walking along the terrace toward them. "Nose to the ground, as always."

"He does look rather as if he's on the trail of something," Tessa agreed uncertainly.

He came straight to their table.

"Mind if I join you?" he asked abruptly, and without waiting for an invitation, he sat down. He brought cigarettes out of his pocket, offered them around and, when they were refused, lit one himself, drawing the smoke deep into his lungs. There was something unusually keyed-up in everything he did. "I've just been hearing things, Mrs. Winfield. Are they true? I mean, about your being attacked in that old mill."

Antonia leaned forward, looking at the hand that was holding the cigarette.

"What a pity mulberry juice looks so like bloodstains," she remarked. "You look just as if you'd come redhanded from committing a crime."

He started, stared at the red stains around his nails and said unsmilingly, "That's right. I didn't notice."

"I suppose you heard the story from Mr. Apodiacos,"

Antonia said. "He's generous with his mulberries."

"Is that his name? Fat little chap with a lot of kids. Yes, he told me."

"And you came rushing here straightaway to find out if there'd been any developments?"

"Well, have there?" he asked.

"Not that I know of."

"They haven't traced the woman, or got the belt back?"

"If they have, they haven't told me so."

A muscle began to twitch under one of his eyes. He put the tips of his fingers against it, trying to hold it still. "And all she took was a belt, just an ordinary belt?"

"It wasn't at all an ordinary belt," Antonia said. "It was a very unusual one, which unluckily didn't belong to me, but to my niece. It's correct, however, that it's all the woman took."

Stanley Smith turned to Tessa. "What do you think about it, Mrs. Foley? Was this unusual belt valuable in any way?"

Instead of answering his question, she remarked, as if to no one in particular, "Inspector Smith interrogates witnesses. Scene Three in Murder in the Old Mill."

His face went a dusky red. "Sorry. Not my business, is that what you mean? Perfectly true. But it sounded quite a story and even though I'm on holiday, I couldn't resist trying to find out a bit more. Force of habit, I'm afraid. I apologize."

"A story? Are you a journalist?" Tessa asked.

"Yes, but I didn't mean to ply my trade while I was here," he said. "It just happens to be one of the things that's difficult to stop. Your mind gets conditioned."

"The odd thing is," Tessa went on, "I'd made up my mind you were an actor."

He gave a self-conscious laugh. "Whatever made you think that?"

"Oh, something about your voice and the way you use your hands—things like that. And the way you started that interrogation. Pure television, I thought."

"As a matter of fact, I was an actor for a time," he said. "No good though. I'm no good at so many things, you'd be surprised. In fact, finding out all the things I'm no good at has been my one steady career. There was a time when I tried helping out in the family pub, the one my parents took over when my father got out of the army. You wouldn't think I could go wrong in that, would you? But my father said I kept the customers away. He said there was something about me that made them nervous. The best living I ever made was as a window cleaner. A pound an hour, if people were desperate enough, and every woman's face lit up with welcome when I came round."

"Why didn't you stick to it?" Antonia asked. "It must have satisfied your tendency to interest yourself in other people's lives."

He went on looking at Tessa. "Just by looking at your aunt, Mrs. Foley, no one would ever guess what damned things she can say, would they? It was the weather that put a stop to it, Mrs. Winfield. When it's fine there's more work than you can cope with, but when there's rain and fog no one's got any use for you and you realize there's a lot to be said for a steady job."

"And what paper have you got this steady job with?" Tessa asked.

"No paper at all. I work for a news agency, the European News Service."

Antonia wished that she could believe him. It was a neat explanation and covered almost everything and would be so reassuring, if it were true. For if only he had been chasing her because he had mistaken her for some newsworthy person, such as the mistress of a bank robber who had got away with the loot, or of a multiple murderer whom she was supposed to have come abroad to join, she wouldn't mind how much he hung about, watching her. No bank robber or murderer would turn up and probably it would dawn on him at last that the tip on which he had followed her had been no good and he would take himself off. And even if he didn't, it wouldn't matter much, if all that he wanted was to write her life story.

But she had never heard of the European News Service.

He and Tessa went on talking. She told him that she herself had once had ideas of being an actress, then she tried to probe a little further into this phase of his life.

If she did it to test him, her suspicions were soon allayed by the discovery that they had mutual acquaintances. Her voice grew warmer; his on the other hand, became more casual, as if he were feeling less anxious about the impression that he was making. Antonia, only half-listening, was aware that soon Tessa was doing most of the talking, moreover was finding a wonderful release in it. There was a sparkle about her that had been quite absent during the last few days. Did it mean so much to her then, this sort of gossip? To Antonia it sounded mainly a matter of name-dropping with a veneer of technical comment. But was it something that Tessa had been missing badly, living with Alec?

Antonia began to consider a new theory of what might have gone wrong between them. She remembered that Roger had always thought that Tessa had been wrong to give up acting, that she had some genuine talent for it and that if she did not use the talent, she was bound to regret it. Not that Antonia knew how Alec would feel if Tessa wanted to resume a career on the stage. He might be all for it. Most of the men whom Antonia knew whose wives were gainfully employed were only too keen that they should keep their noses to the grindstone. Against that it was always easier to imagine Alec opposing, rather than supporting, almost anything you could think of.

Anyway, Tessa's conversation with Stanley Smith was becoming so interesting to them both that Antonia half-expected her to invite him to join them at dinner. But she did not, and afterward, when he seemed to assume that they would go on from where they had broken off, Tessa eluded him and sat down on the terrace with Dave Lambrick and his chessboard. Seeing the glazed stare of the dedicated chess player settle on her face, Antonia went up to bed, thinking how lucky it was that Tessa had this passion for the game, because it felt far safer to leave her with the American, with his nice, sensitive face and informativeness about flowering shrubs, than with Stanley Smith.

In the night the wind died down. The crashing of the waves on the beach sank to a little whisper of sound. The foam came swishing delicately up the sand, then was sucked softly back into the dark calm. In the morning the sea was all gentle invitation. The sky was cloudless and the distances faded into a shimmering haze. Antonia and Tessa spent most of the day on the beach. They swam, lay on the sand in the sun or in the shade of a beach umbrella, read and did not talk much. Antonia almost deluded herself that everything was normal and just as she had hoped that it would be. Sun and sea are a powerful combination, almost compelling the mind to be at peace. She yielded to them as she might have to a drug that was pulling her mind toward oblivion.

But suddenly an unexpected question from Tessa startled her out of her semi-comatose state.

"Antonia, tell me something—what are your ideas about the bomb?"

"The—?" Antonia had heard the question perfectly well,

but it was so foreign to the mistiness in her mind just then that it knocked her thoughts sprawling.

"The bomb," Tessa repeated. "Do you think the human race is going to destroy itself completely in a little while?"

"For heaven's sake, why ask *me* a thing like that?" Antonia demanded.

"The problem affects you just as much as everyone else," Tessa answered.

"And I can do just as little about it," Antonia said. "Tessa, you'd better be a bit careful with that fair skin of yours. You don't want to get blistered all over."

Tessa rolled over into the shade of the umbrella. She rested her chin on her folded arms.

"I'd really like to know what you think," she said earnestly.

"I suppose I think that if it weren't for the bomb we'd all have been at each other's throats again in another outburst of conventionality just a bit worse than the last one," Antonia said. "But how much longer we'll go on being frightened enough of the bomb to stand any more peace, I don't know."

"I wish you'd be serious," Tessa said.

"Look, you know what I'm like about politics," Antonia said. "When someone comes to the door, collecting for a jumble sale, I give them something, regardless of party. And don't look so shocked. It's a way of supporting the system in general and I'd never get rid of Roger's old suits otherwise. Apart from that, a good chunk of my life was spent fussing rather futilely about other bombs, so I expect my emotions have got a bit calloused. You're young, so it obviously looks quite different to you."

As she stopped, Tessa lowered her face into her arms and remained silent.

Antonia suddenly realized how stupid she had just been.

Tessa hadn't wanted her to talk, she had only wanted her to make the right noises to show that she was ready to listen, because the impulse had come to Tessa at last to talk about those "political" difficulties between herself and Alec that she had mentioned in Athens. But Antonia had made the wrong noises. That was certain, for although she waited now, Tessa did not speak again. After a little while, Antonia got to her feet, saying that she felt like another bathe, and left her.

Later in the day she had a talk with Mrs. Marinatos. This was a necessary part of her plan and she had thought out carefully beforehand what she wanted to say. She explained that some friends of hers were leaving Athens that day to drive up to Salonika, that they didn't want to break their journey for as long as they would have to if they came to the island, but had said that if she and her niece would meet them on the mainland, they could all have a day or two together.

"So that's what we've decided to do," Antonia said. "We'll leave tomorrow and come back on Friday—that's when the ship calls again, isn't it?—and we'd like to keep our rooms on while we're gone."

The manageress fidgeted with some forms on the table before her, put some pens straight, then gave a strained smile.

"Certainly, if you wish it," she said. "But I'm sure you have no need to fear a repetition of what happened yesterday, Mrs. Winfield. It was very regrettable and everyone here is very sorry for it, but our police will find the woman. You may be quite secure."

"Ah, that isn't our reason for going, not at all," Antonia said, though she did not mind in the least if Mrs. Marinatos continued to believe that it was and spread it around among the other guests, so that it reached Stanley Smith.

"Shall I order a taxi to take you to the ship?" Mrs. Marinatos asked. "You can have lunch here early and leave at one o'clock. But if you prefer to go by the bus, you must be ready at twelve forty-five."

"Thank you, I think we'll go by the bus and have lunch on the ship," Antonia answered. For if they left by taxi, when the bus had already gone, and if the other taxi on the island happened to have been engaged by somebody else, it might actually be impossible for Stanley Smith to follow them. And in that case nothing would be proved. They might escape from him, if they were ready to continue with some fancy dodging about the Greek mainland, but she would be no nearer to convincing Tessa, or anyone else, that he really was on her trail.

Next day the two of them went to wait for the bus at the hotel entrance a full quarter of an hour before it was due. Most of the other guests were sitting on the terrace, waiting for lunch. Mr. Mobey went by with a loaf under his arm and his string bag full of vegetables. Mr. Apodiacos strolled past and waved to them. Dave Lambrick, looking rather aggrieved, as if he felt that Tessa ought to have told him that she was leaving, came to talk to her and helped her and Antonia with their suitcases when the bus came. But Stanley Smith was nowhere to be seen.

The ship was in the harbor already when the bus drew up on the quay and the launches had put off from the shore some minutes before to pick up the passengers who were leaving the ship. The big man in charge of the weighing machine was waiting to grab the luggage of some unsuspecting tourist and scare the wits out of him by making him believe that he had failed to comply with one of the fundamental laws of the Greek nation. One of the taxis arrived empty and drew up alongside the bus, waiting for custom. Antonia met Tessa's eyes and shrugged. Her plan had failed. Just when she did not want to do so, she was going to escape from Stanley Smith.

But just then, when the first of the launches was almost at the quayside, the second taxi drove up and Stanley Smith leaped out. Antonia saw with satisfaction that he looked more agitated, more hot and breathless than she had ever seen him. It had been a near thing for him. If she had been worried at losing him, he had been far more worried at nearly losing her.

She heard Tessa draw a long breath when she saw him. She said in a low voice, "I'm sorry—of course I ought to have known you were right all along. What do you want to do now? Do you still want to go away, or shall I go and tell him straightaway that if he doesn't get on this ship and leave we'll go to the police and complain about him? Both of us together. That's what you wanted, isn't it?"

"Just a minute," Antonia said.

She was looking at the launch that had just arrived with its unsteady-looking heap of luggage in the stern and its load of passengers.

"I think—well—I rather expect we may want to change all our plans now," she said quietly.

For among the new arrivals were both Alec and Roger.

# CHAPTER NINE

Alec looked hot and tired in one of his dark suits that did not really fit him, but which had come through the journey as neatly, as doggedly formal as always. There were blue circles under his eyes and he had the wincing, half-blind stare of someone with a bad headache.

Roger, tall, spare, erect, in a wilted shirt and shapeless flannel trousers that were threatening to slither down over his lean hips, did not look tired at all. But he almost never did. If his thin face, with its big prow of a nose, its bony forehead and long jaw never had much color, it never lost what it had. His skin, which had been netted with fine wrinkles for almost as long as Antonia could remember, never sagged, never went puffy from weariness. His eyes became dull only when he was bored.

He and Antonia embraced and kissed.

Tessa and Alec walked toward one another, stood still about a yard apart and muttered some sort of greeting, both avoiding a direct look into the other's face.

At the same moment Stanley Smith darted forward into

the crowd on the quay and seized by the hand a short, burly man with a pouchy, heavily veined face and a splendid mop of gray hair that fell forward over his forehead in wind-tossed ringlets. They both gave cries of delight in Italian, pumped their hands up and down, clapped one another's shoulders and went off together to the taxi in which Stanley Smith had arrived.

Tessa looked at Antonia.

Antonia turned her head away, pretending not to notice. She knew what the look meant. It meant that Tessa was against her again. She no longer believed that Stanley Smith had come to the harbor because he was following them. It had only been to meet a friend.

Smiling up at Roger, Antonia said, "This is a very nice surprise. I suppose there's probably some reason why you're here that isn't particularly nice, but I'm glad all the same."

Out of the corner of her eye she saw that Smith and his friend had not got into their taxi. They were standing beside it, talking. Wasn't that because they were taking no chances? They were waiting to see whether or not she and Tessa were still going to leave the island in spite of the arrival of their husbands.

"Tell you all about it presently," Roger said. He was looking at the suitcases. "You weren't just leaving, were you? I thought you were going to roost here for three weeks."

"Oh, we were just going for a short excursion," Antonia answered. "We'll drop it, since you're here. Quick, grab that taxi—no, too late." For the empty taxi had just been taken. "And I'm afraid there aren't any more."

"Never mind, we can walk," Roger said, picking up her suitcase as well as his own. "How far is it?"

She cried out in horror, "Miles!" She wondered if the

day would ever come when Roger ceased to assume that the simplest way of getting from one place to another was on his feet, furthermore, that if he were sufficiently breezy about it, she could be brought to the same view of the matter. "No, we'll take the bus. And if the man over there with the weighing machine wants to weigh your luggage and nobody else's and you don't find that reasonable, just let him weigh it all the same and don't make a fuss."

"Good," Roger said. "I was afraid you were going to tell me I'd have to make a fuss and were going to be disappointed in me. This heat takes all the aggression out of one."

However, today the man with the weighing machine was smoking a cigarette and laughing richly over a story that he himself was telling with much dramatic gesture to a circle of friends and the luggage was all safely stowed on top of the bus without his interference.

Inside the bus Tessa and Alec sat stiffly side by side, looking in different directions. Antonia and Roger sat behind them.

"Well now, tell me why you've come," Antonia said as the bus started. She wondered if Tessa had noticed that it was only when it started that the taxi with Stanley Smith and his friend in it had begun to move. "Was it because of . . . ?" She gestured at the two in the seat in front of them.

"Yes and no," Roger answered. "I had to go back to London because the police wanted me. We had a burglary."

"We—us—our house?" She stared at him.

"Yes, the night you left. Someone broke in by the front door. It was a simple, crude job with a jimmy, smashing the lock. He rummaged through the house, then got disturbed by the chap on the beat who noticed the door wasn't shut properly. So our man did a bolt down to the basement, got out through the kitchen and went over the garden wall and got away."

"What did he take?" Antonia asked.

"Nothing that I could see, that's the odd thing about it. But it was hard to say for sure. I suppose I'm reasonably well acquainted with our possessions, and if the burglar had left something of his own behind, I expect I'd have spotted it and known it wasn't ours. But it's a much more difficult test of the memory to decide if something that's usually there has suddenly gone missing." He thought over this statement and decided that it wasn't quite accurate. "Of course I don't mean something like a carpet or a piano."

"But what about the silver and so on?" Antonia asked.

"None of it touched, so far as I could tell. The first thing I looked at was that jewel-box thing of yours and a few odds and ends seemed to be missing, but I thought you'd probably got them with you."

"Yes, I did bring two or three things," she said.

"After all, it didn't seem likely that a man in a hurry would carefully pick out a few special items, none of them of any great value, and leave the rest. He'd probably tip the lot into his pockets and go. Same thing with the silver. So whatever he was looking for, he seems to have been disappointed."

"Did he make an awful mess of the place?"

"Not too bad. It was mainly the bedrooms that he turned upside down. He did a certain amount of hunting through drawers and cupboards all over the house, but it was our bedroom he really went to work on. It's all rather mysterious and looks as if he must have been misinformed about us. It looked, you see, as if he'd been hunting for something special, or so the police think. It definitely wasn't a case of a man just strolling by, seeing a house

111

without lights and trying his luck. It seems to have been planned. They found out that a man had been seen hanging round the place for the last day or two. Several people saw him. Their descriptions of him varied a good deal, as I imagine they always do, but the general picture was that he was a thin sort of chap, with dark hair and a shabby brown suit—"

"Darling!" Antonia cried. She clutched his arm as if it were a rope that had just been thrown to her to draw her to safety. Her face lit up with a smile of wonderful brilliance. "A man in a brown suit—oh, darling Roger!"

"Yes. Well. Hm. Yes, of course." Eying her with astonishment, he cleared his throat and patted her hand. "As I was saying . . . What the devil *was* I saying? Antonia, my dear, there's nothing wrong, is there?"

"An awful lot is wrong," she said, "but not nearly as wrong as it was a moment ago."

"You actually seem pleased about this burglary."

"I'm delighted. I'm . . . No, it's too complicated to tell you about just now, I'll tell you the whole thing presently. Go on about why you came here."

"Well, I got your telegram," he said. "It went to Edinburgh, of course, and had to be sent on after me, so it only reached me on Saturday. But as soon as I got it, I got in touch with Alec." He dropped his voice, though the bus was filled with such a clatter of ancient machinery that this was hardly necessary. "He was in a pretty bad way, feeling he owed it to himself to do something violent and dramatic, but not quite knowing what. So when we'd talked for a bit, it seemed to me the best thing all round was for us to come out here after you. Alec had two weeks of holiday due to him and he managed to fix it up. I hope it wasn't an appalling blunder."

"For them? I don't know and at the moment I don't

care. For me nothing could have been more right. I'll explain what I mean later. Let's have a talk after lunch, somewhere where we can't be interrupted."

She was thinking of their bedroom, which luckily was a double room, so there would be no problem about Roger's moving in with her. Tessa had a double room also, but it was unlikely, Antonia thought, that she and Alec would agree to share it. She was taken by surprise, therefore, when they reached the hotel, to learn that they had arranged between them to do this. Tessa's manner, when she mentioned it, suggested that she didn't mind who shared her room, that it was a matter of complete indifference to her and that anyone who was short of a bed would have been equally welcome. Alec's tired face showed neither satisfaction nor dismay. But at least their agreement saved awkward discussion with the manageress, who was bewildered enough already at the prompt return of her two guests with unexpected husbands.

At the late lunch served for the new arrivals, they had the dining room to themselves except for Stanley Smith and the Italian whom he had brought back from the ship and another newcomer, a sour-faced, elderly Frenchman, who looked as if he were sure that everything he ate would disagree with him.

Afterward, Antonia suggested to Roger that they should go to their room. She wanted to take off her shoes and her girdle, lie down and have their talk in comfort. She ought to have known that there was no hope of Roger agreeing. His idea of the best way to aid the digestion of a heavy meal was to go for a ten-mile walk. A stroll, he called it, a breath of air. Twenty years ago Antonia might have been fooled. Now there was no more chance of his getting her to attempt it than there was of persuading Roger to take a siesta. They wrangled quietly for a little while, then agreed on the compromise of going for a drive.

There was only one drive that they could take unless they wanted to return to the harbor. Only one of the tracks that wound away into the hills to the other side of the island was like enough to a road for a car to be driven along it. Even it had a surface of deep clogging dust and was thickly strewn with small rocks. The driver, who looked a brigand of a man, with wild dark eyes and several front teeth missing, and who could easily have been the descendant of one of the pirates who had caused the peaceful inhabitants of the island to build their homes "upstairs," drove with great skill, however. He knew every bump in the road like a well-loved friend, and waved his hand at hilltops and diminutive churches, at vistas of rock and pine and distant sea, inviting Roger and Antonia to admire and enjoy, which they would most willingly have done if they had had the power—while they were being jolted up and down and flung from side to side in the car—to take proper notice of what he was pointing out to them. They gave up any idea of trying to talk until they had reached the point where they had arranged that he was to put them down, then pick them up again in an hour's time.

This was on some flat ground above a small cove, so enclosed by pine-covered hills that the reflections of the trees in the motionless water gave it the tint of those pieces of old bottle glass that have been thrown into the sea and gradually burnished by the waves and the sand to jewel-like smoothness. There were some very small cottages along the shore and there was one fishing boat in the cove, on which some men were packing great crabs into baskets. The air was warmly scented with the resin of the pines.

Roger and Antonia strolled along a path that ran behind the cottages, then along beside a dried-up stream, which soon lost itself among the trees. Most of the trees had had slivers of bark cut from their trunks and small wedge-shaped cans fastened at the base of the cuts to catch the resin that oozed out. Some of the tins were brimming over with the sticky, grayish fluid, presently to be used for flavoring retsina, and thick with dead flies. Great clumps of oleanders grew among the boulders in the bed of the stream.

In a comfortable hollow softly carpeted with pine needles and not beset by too many ants, Roger and Antonia sat down and leaned their backs against the trunk of a tree. The air throbbed with the sound of cicadas, and a small lizard came out from under a stone to look at them.

"Now," Roger said, "what's all the trouble about? Not Tessa and Alec. You said there's something else."

"Lots else." She picked up a handful of pine needles and let them dribble away through her fingers. "To start with, did you notice those two men at the corner table in the dining room?"

"I noticed they were there," Roger said. "I didn't pay much attention to them."

"Next time you see them, then, take a very good look at the thin dark one, because he's our burglar."

Roger raised an eyebrow. "I suppose that isn't just a wild guess. You really know something."

"Oh yes," she said. "Let me tell you the whole thing. It began at our bus stop at home, last Tuesday morning. He was waiting for a bus and I mistook him for Jack Singer, that technician of yours, and nearly spoke to him, then realized I was wrong and didn't. But that's how I happened to notice him. If I hadn't made that mistake, he could have turned up here and it would never have occurred to me I'd seen him before. . . ."

She went on with the story.

Fortunately Roger was someone who was capable of listening attentively for quite a long time while another person spoke. He had never been one of the people who feel that the quickest way to get to the bottom of something is to do all the talking themselves. He did not keep popping in questions and comments that made her lose the thread of her story.

When she finished, his silence continued for a time. He was watching the lizard flicking in and out among the sun-warmed stones near his feet.

At last he observed, "You haven't exactly said so, but I've a feeling that the thing that's really worrying is where Tessa fits into all this."

She shook her head. "No . . . Unless you mean the way I haven't been able to make her take me seriously. Of course that's worried me a great deal."

"I meant the question of how far she's involved with Smith," Roger said, "because there's something rather odd about the time sequence. Let's begin at the end and work backwards. Someone stole your belt. Tessa's belt. Someone also broke into our house, but appears to have stolen nothing. It doesn't seem unreasonable then to think that it may have been the belt he was after. Let's not bother about the reason why. We can come back to that later. Whatever it was, it was important enough to make him take off immediately for Greece, to try to pick Tessa up on the boat and to do his Romeo act at her balcony. But meanwhile Tessa had given the belt to you. And he knew you were onto him. So he had to get hold of someone else to do the job of following you and stealing the belt and he got the woman in black. It all seems to fit quite nicely, only there's one great big snag. It's the fact that Smith started following you about and watching the house before there was any suggestion of Tessa going away with you, or even that she might be coming to stay with you."

Antonia nodded. "That's what Tessa said herself."

"So however unwilling to consider it we may feel, it looks very much as if Tessa's somehow involved in the thing, because somehow Smith knew what she was going to do before you did."

"I just don't believe it," Antonia said. "Tessa's entirely honest. One just knows that. She's been all prickles ever since she turned up, she's made it quite clear she didn't want me to probe into her affairs, but I'm sure that's only because she's determined not to be influenced by anyone when she makes up her mind about Alec. It isn't because she'd cooked up something mysterious beforehand with this man Smith."

"Tell me something," Roger said. "When Tessa came to us, had she her passport with her? Was she prepared for going abroad?"

"I don't know. I haven't thought about it. Anyway, she'd time to go back to the flat and get it while Alec was at the office."

"A pity. If she'd had it with her, it might have told us something important."

"Not necessarily. A passport's something one would probably grab and stick in one's bag if one thought one was leaving a place forever."

"Perhaps it is. All the same, there's a thing to remember —Smith let you get away in Farr's only when he'd made quite sure where you were going. If he knew that Tessa would be coming to us, if he knew that she'd have the belt with her, if he knew there was a good probability that she'd go abroad with you—"

She interrrupted. "That would mean Tessa didn't know what he was up to, wouldn't it?"

"Possibly it would."

"Yet he got his information from someone."

"Unless he isn't involved in the theft of the belt. If he hadn't the information that Tessa was coming to Hampstead, I don't think it's possible that he was involved in the theft of the belt. He's up to something certainly, but it's something else."

"And the woman in black was really just a crazy creature who thought I was wearing a lot of money round my waist and couldn't resist it."

"Only you're still sure she wasn't."

"Oh, Roger, I don't know! With the Smith business so much on my mind I simply panicked when I realized I was being followed by someone else as well. Then I saw the girl from Athens and she had those great alarming black eyes and I instantly decided she was the woman. But I'd really nothing to go on and I was in a horrid state of nerves, so I could easily have been quite wrong. But if there is a connection between her and Smith it helps to explain her treatment of her unfortunate fiancé, doesn't it? I mean, if she'd had instructions from Smith by telephone to keep an eye on us till he could get to Greece himself, it would explain why she insisted on sitting in the lobby by herself, watching the door, and why she insisted on going to that hotel that evening, and why she keeps disappearing now to visit friends with sick mothers."

"Returning to the subject of Tessa," Roger said, "hasn't she said anything at all about why she's left Alec?"

"Not much."

"You don't think it's a question of another man?"

"I don't *think* so."

"I was just wondering if that's where Smith fits in."

She shook her head. "Another woman perhaps. Whatever it is, it's something that she blames Alec for. She's angry with him, and she doesn't feel guilty herself. But the only thing she's actually told me is that it's 'in a sense political.' I think that's what she said. Then she said she was only talking nonsense. Then yesterday she suddenly started asking me what I thought about the bomb and wanting to know if I thought the human race was shortly going to be destroyed, and somehow I feel fairly sure it all had something to do with Alec."

"It almost sounds as if she's worrying that he's turned Communist," Roger said. "Funny—I'd swear he had all the makings of an arch-Conservative. Not that I really know anything about him. Perhaps it's Tessa who's got the bug and she can't forgive him for not being converted likewise. That's more likely, I should think. There's that queer disorganized streak in her which might make the idea of revolutions very attractive. Temporarily, anyway."

"I don't think so. I think she meant something else. But what are we going to do about Stanley Smith, Roger?"

"Follow a shadow, it still flies you. Seem to fly it, it will pursue. . . ."

"What do you mean?"

He did not answer at once. Indeed, he took so long to answer that Antonia, who had been gazing into the distance, where a blue thread of sea showed between the pines, turned her head to look at him.

She saw that quite suddenly he had fallen asleep.

# CHAPTER TEN

His face had gone slack and his mouth had dropped a little open. Antonia let him go on sleeping.

The time passed at which they had agreed with the driver to return to the car. The shadows on the ground lengthened a little and some of the power went out of the heat of the sun. Near at hand there was a sound of children's voices. Roger gave one very loud snore and woke up.

"As I was saying . . ." he began. Then, waking more fully, he laughed at himself and said, "Time to be moving, isn't it?"

They got up and started back along the path beside the dried-up stream.

Three boys, the children whom Antonia had heard, were at a well, filling some earthenware jars with water. On a hillock behind them a man was winnowing corn. He had on the usual baggy blue trousers and leggings and had his head tied up in a sort of turban to keep the chaff out of his hair. With the sun behind him, lighting up grain and chaff as he tossed them into the air with a rhythmic swing of the fork, he was all enveloped in a golden cloud.

As Roger and Antonia walked on, the children trotted barefooted behind them. They were accompanied by a small, friendly dog that came sniffing around the Winfields' ankles. When Antonia paused to pat it, the children also paused, looking at her and Roger from a slight distance with deep curiosity and diffident smiles. They were far shier than the children in the town on the hill.

Two women were waiting for them at the gate of one of the cottages. It was a very small cottage in the middle of a big garden filled with sunflowers in full bloom. One of the women started to speak to Roger and Antonia. She was very thin and dark, was dressed in a bright red blouse and an emerald-green skirt, very much frayed at the hem, and was carrying a water jar on her shoulder. She smiled as she spoke, showing gums with only a few blackened teeth, but the smile had an animation that gave a vivid charm to her bony brown face, although she had only one eye.

She gestured at the gate of the cottage. The other woman held it open and smiled too. She was the older of the two, the smaller and the plumper, with a round, gentle face and the calmest of gray eyes. She also waved invitingly toward the cottage, while the dark woman began to repeat what she had said.

Antonia responded with a regretful smile and said in an apologetic tone that she did not understand Greek.

The dark woman laughed and went on, implying that understanding would come if they would only try.

This time, in the midst of all the words that meant nothing to her, Antonia caught one that did. She said to Roger, "I believe we're being asked in to have coffee."

"How nice. Then let's go in," he said.

"What about the taxi? We're late already."

"We'll deal with that problem when we get to it."

Antonia turned back to the two women, smiled and nodded and went up the path between the sunflowers to the white cottage.

It turned out to be the home of the older woman. When they reached it, it was she who set chairs for them all on the small vine-covered terrace, who put water to boil in a black cauldron on a wood fire that was smoldering on the ground near them, who brought out three tiny coffee cups, one for each of her guests but none for herself, and started to make the coffee in a little copper pot.

While she was doing it the three boys settled down in a heap in a corner of the terrace, all entwined, like a litter of puppies, with three pairs of eyes fixed unblinkingly on Roger and Antonia.

There followed one of the oddest conversations in which either of them had ever been involved, for somehow they all talked a great deal and laughed a great deal and yet the only spoken language that they had in common was the small amount of Greek that Antonia had memorized from her phrase book and about the same amount of Italian, learned by her in the same way and by the other women from the soldiers quartered in this remote place during the war, when they must both have been children. But the one-eyed woman had a wonderfully expressive face and voice and a command of gesture that made speech almost unnecessary, and Roger was surprisingly quick at understanding this kind of communication and skillful at miming replies, which the woman appeared to find perfectly clear. And if in fact they were talking about quite different things, none of them would ever find it out, so what did it matter?

To tell them how she had lost her eye, the one-eyed woman scratched with a fingernail at the white limewash on the wall of the cottage, made gestures of painting, then pointed at the eye. Roger and Antonia made shocked noises of sympathy. The woman shrugged them off, laughed, reached out to a clump of marguerites growing near her, picked two and tucked one behind Antonia's ear and one behind Roger's. Everyone laughed then, even the three solemn boys. The older woman, satisfied with the success of her party, wandered a little way off into her garden and started picking flowers too. She picked quantities of roses, carnations and lemon-scented geraniums and returned to give them to Antonia.

The only difficulty arose after her gift of the flowers, when she had the idea of giving Roger and Antonia some eggs to take away with them. They shook their heads and said, "No, thank you." Troubled, the woman said, "*Simera! Simera!*"—meaning "today," and that the eggs were fresh. They shook their heads again. But how could they explain that they were staying in a hotel where they were already overfed and in any case had no cooking facilities? The woman started wrapping the eggs up in squares of newspaper, and it was only when the one-eyed woman, who had the quicker understanding, checked her quietly that she desisted.

Roger then took his camera out of its case, pointed it at the three boys and looked inquiringly at their mother for her permission to take a photograph of them.

At once the beautiful heap of young arms and legs disintegrated. The boys jumped to their feet and stood in a straight row with solemn, hang-dog faces. Their mother tut-tutted at the holes in their clothes and smoothed their hair. It was a great pity, but there was nothing to be done about it, since neither Roger nor Antonia knew how to ask the boys to go back to where they had been before. Roger photographed them as they were, then took the notebook and pencil from his pocket and managed to convey to their mother that he would like her name and address, so that he could send her prints of the pictures. While he was carefully writing down what she spelled out to him, the children lost their rigor, dropped to hands and knees again and, with their faces bright with interest, clustered around him to watch him write his own strange language.

When the Winfields left, after many times repeating the only words of thanks that they knew, they were both in the grip of an intense regret that something that had happened to them so surprisingly, so charmingly, just when they had been tying their minds into knots with worry, should so quickly be over. As they walked on they suddenly found themselves quite without words, even in English.

The taxi driver had not only waited for them quite happily but was not yet ready to leave the place himself. He was on the boat in the cove negotiating with the fishermen for a basket of monstrous crabs. When the deal was concluded and he returned to the taxi, he showed the Winfields his load, gave a gluttonous grin that showed every one of his few teeth, patted his stomach, tilted his head back, and made a gurgling sound.

"Retsina!" he said.

In the taxi on the way back to the hotel, Roger observed, "I wonder why human beings bothered to invent speech."

He had forgotten about the marguerite tucked behind his ear and Antonia did not remind him of it until they were almost back at the hotel. When she did, he became self-conscious at once and removed it, but it was a moment before he could bring himself to drop the flower.

In the hotel, when Antonia had put her bunch of flowers in water in their bedroom, she and Roger went looking for Tessa and Alec. They found them on the terrace. Alec for once was in a shirt and shorts instead of a suit. Thickset, firm-muscled, in a stiff attitude of angry pride, he looked rather handsomer than usual, but decidedly not quite safe to have around. He and Tessa were talking in low voices, very intent on one another, with empty glasses on the table before them and also what looked, from a slight distance, like a heap of golden coins. Tessa looked up with a start as Roger and Antonia came toward them, then gathered up the pile of gold in one hand and held it out to Antonia.

"Here you are," she said. "Your belt. It's come back safely."

"What happened?" Roger asked as he and Antonia sat down.

"The police came here with it while you were gone," Tessa said, "and gave it back to me. Here . . ." She was still holding it out to Antonia.

"Thank you, but I think you'd better keep it now," Antonia said. She had seen Alec's quick scowl. It hurt him that Tessa had even lent it to her. "It doesn't seem to have luck with me. Did the police tell you anything about where they found it?"

"They said a child found it this afternoon and brought it to them," Tessa said. "She found it under a bush somewhere, as if it had been thrown away."

"Then perhaps we ought to give her a reward," Antonia suggested. "Roger, don't you think so?"

In a dull tone, as if he had no interest in the conversation, Alec said, "I've attended to that already."

"Oh, thank you," Antonia said. She wished that she could somehow immunize herself against the undercurrent of hostility that she always heard in his voice. It set her against him even when she wanted most to protect his feelings. "And what about the woman who took it? Have they found out anything about her?"

"She's a stranger, that's all they know for certain," Tessa said. "But a lot of people seem to have noticed her. They noticed her simply because she was a stranger. I suppose that's bound to happen in a place where everybody knows everybody. Several people thought there was something odd about her too. But now she's vanished into thin air. The last person who saw her was the man who was driving some donkeys along the path behind you when you were going to the windmill."

"And who stopped her snatching the belt there and then," Antonia said. "I was so thankful at the time, but perhaps it was a pity. If she'd done it then, I'd at least have seen where she went to afterwards. Did the police tell you if they're still looking for her, or have they given her up, now that they've found the belt?"

"I suppose they're still looking for her," Tessa said.

"I wonder if they've asked those two Germans about her. They were out swimming near the windmill when she vanished."

"They didn't say anything about that."

The Germans were sitting on the terrace near them. Antonia considered going over to them to question them herself. But as usual they had their heads close together and were talking so earnestly and with so little awareness of anyone near them that she gave up the idea. She thought that probably, even when they were swimming in a rough sea, they would still have been talking on and on to one another and a giantess in black could have passed them by without their noticing.

Near them sat the Frenchman who had arrived that day. He had a glass of ouzo before him, from which he took an occasional sip, screwing up his lips afterward as if he found it almost unbearably repellent.

At the table next to him sat Mrs. Ball, who had made friends with the young man from Glasgow, who was just then saying with anxious solemnity, "I apologize—I apologize very sincerely indeed—for intruding on you with my private affairs, and I thank you for your understanding. It relieves me that you think I have a problem. It takes a great weight off my mind. You see, I don't want to seem unreasonable or demanding. I worship the ground that girl walks on. But there are times when I begin to wonder if this marriage is going to work out as I hoped."

"What marriage ever does?" Mrs. Ball asked kindly. "But what I actually said, Mr. McDougal, was that your fiancée has a problem. She isn't well adjusted. She needs help."

"But that's what I keep telling her," Mr. McDougal protested. "I keep saying to her when I see her, which isn't often—I haven't seen her since breakfast—'Look,' I say, 'the way you're behaving simply isn't normal, and if it goes on, you'll soon have me right round the bend as well.'"

"Now you'll pardon me, I know," Mrs. Ball said in a tone of great gentleness, "if I tell you that isn't just the best thing you can say to her. You shouldn't let a sensitive girl like that see that you're disturbed about her condition. You should be thinking instead how to interest her in things outside herself."

"But damn it, that's just what I keep trying to do, only she won't let me—" He stopped himself, adding with increased distress, "Madam, I apologize for swearing in your presence. But I've been under a considerable strain recently."

Mrs. Ball gave a forgiving laugh and went on comfortably giving him her advice. It was a very happy accident for her as well as for the young man, Antonia thought, that they had found one another. Each was just what the other needed.

"Now I really must go and look for her," he said as he rose to go. "Perhaps she's been waiting for me all the time round at the back or somewhere. We don't always understand each other as well as we might."

Roger had taken the belt from Tessa and had been looking at it curiously.

"You know, there's something very queer about this thing," he said. "I suppose you noticed it. Someone's had a jolly good try at splitting these coins open."

He showed them what he meant. Some instrument like a fine chisel had been hammered against the edges of several of the coinlike discs and, because they were made of some very soft metal, the end of the tool had dug into them quite easily. It had then been twisted about to open up the slits.

"What a shame," Antonia said. "It's spoilt them."

"Well, there's nothing of interest inside them," Alec said with a sardonic smile. "No heroin, no microfilm. What a bitter disappointment for somebody."

"I think they could be mended," Tessa said, taking the belt from Roger. "All they need is a little hammering to flatten them. I believe I could do it myself."

"Oh, throw the damned thing away!" Alec said with sudden violence, his brown eyes blazing. "You never cared for it anyway."

"Heroin?" Roger said thoughtfully. "Microfilm? Well, well."

Alec began to laugh. It was angry laughter, but his voice was level again when he said, "I'm sorry, that was just a response to the drama in the situation. It didn't mean anything."

"Such a very apt response, though," Roger said gently. "And there *is* a good deal of drama in the air, like it or not. There was our burglary in Hampstead, and there's this business about a man following Antonia round, and there was the theft of this belt."

"But really, professor," Alec said, "if I'd thought you could possibly take me seriously, I'd never have made that idiot remark. No one could imagine—"

"Oh, why can't you call them Roger and Antonia, like everyone else?" Tessa broke in with extraordinary irritation.

"I was going to say," Alec went on, "that no one could imagine Mrs. Winfield—" He hesitated, as if he were trying to make himself say Antonia, then with a firmness that she rather admired, stuck to what came more naturally to him. "No one could imagine Mrs. Winfield being involved in drug smuggling or spying, which is what my silly remark implied."

"Thank you, Alec dear, that's very kind," Antonia said.

His cheeks reddened. "Oh, I'm aware it was a ridiculous thing to say, but our conversation seems to have taken a ridiculous turn."

"Which you started," Tessa said.

"The point is," Roger went on with quiet seriousness, "someone thinks Antonia's involved in something, and whatever it is, this belt seems to be involved in it too, since the first thing they do—whoever 'they' are—when they get hold of it is to prize the coins open. And finding nothing, they throw the belt away. So I think your idea, Alec, isn't one to be rejected out of hand."

"You're remembering that the belt belongs to Tessa," Alec said, "and that it was only by chance that Mrs. Winfield was wearing it?"

"Yes, and that Antonia had already been followed for several days before Tessa suddenly decided she couldn't stand married life any more and walked out," said Roger.

"It wasn't sudden," Tessa said.

"Sudden enough for the purposes of this discussion, I imagine," Roger said. "Certainly Antonia didn't know you meant to descend on her. She hadn't any thought of your going abroad with her. So it's hard to see how that shadow of hers could have had any idea of it either. I'm afraid this promising line of argument breaks down there, unless . . ." He paused, raising his eyebrows as if in surprise at one of his own thoughts.

Antonia filled the pause by observing, " 'I have a little shadow who goes in and out with me, But what can be the use of him is more than I can see.' "

"Unless," Alec said, "Tessa and I are involved. That's what you were going to say, isn't it?"

"Of course not," Roger replied as indifferently as if he and Antonia had not been all over this ground earlier in the day and he had not been leading up to this point deliberately to see how Alec would respond. "I was going to say, the argument breaks down unless Antonia's right that she's been followed by mistake and the person for whom she's been mistaken really was smuggling something abroad inside a belt of gold coins."

"That would mean the coincidences were rather piling up on top of one another, wouldn't it?" Alec said. "Two women who can be mistaken for one another *and* two belts."

"Yes, it is a bit much," Roger agreed. "But have you a better explanation?"

"Not at present."

"Well then, until we find a better hypothesis, I think I'll stick to it. And the first thing that strikes me is that Mrs. X, smuggler or spy, is liable to have not just Mr. Smith at her heels, but a whole pack of other people too. There'd be the people with whom she was supposed to make contact to deliver the goods. And there might be some other people who'd be trying to get to her first to steal whatever it is she's got with her. And, of course, the law of we don't know quite how many countries."

"But then—" Antonia gave a startled look up and down the terrace. She saw the Frenchman, the two Germans, the American woman and now there was quiet Dave Lambrick, too, who had just settled down at a table and was setting up his chessboard. "But then *any* of these people . . ."

"Exactly," Roger said.

"Except that they'd all have had to make the same absurd mistake as my Mr. Smith," she said, "and how could they have done that?"

"How did Smith do it?" Roger asked. "That's a question of some importance. There's also the question of what's happened to Mrs. X, and who she is."

"And there's another one," Alec said. "Now that he—they—whoever it is, knows that the belt the woman took wasn't the one they wanted, what will they do next?"

Tessa suddenly jumped to her feet. "I can't stand this!" Her voice was shrilly out of control. But as she saw heads along the terrace turn toward her, she took a deep breath and started again. "I can't stand this," she said in a harsh whisper. "None of you believes what you're saying. I don't know why you trouble to say it. You all know Stanley Smith hasn't been following Antonia. If he's been following anyone, he's been following me."

Alec made a quick gesture, as if to quiet her. She stepped back out of his reach.

"Would it interest you to know that he *told* me he'd been following me?" she said. "He told me that our first night here. He came to my balcony when I was sitting out on it, dreaming about—about all sorts of things, and he told me a stupid story about seeing me in Athens and feeling he had to follow me."

"Only in Athens?" Roger said. "Not in London?"

"No, but of course it began in London. And he only said it at all in case I'd spotted him before he talked to me on the ship. He only followed Antonia to find out where she was going, because he knew I might be going with her. I know she didn't know that herself, and nor did I. But, you see, my leaving Alec *wasn't* so very sudden. He'd known it was coming, just as I had. And he knew I'd probably go to her, and also that she'd be going abroad. So he thought it all out. Alec's very good at thinking things out. He's awfully clever—in some ways. And he put Stanley Smith on my trail—a detective, a miserable private detective—because he wouldn't believe I could possibly think of leaving him unless I was going to another man. As if I wouldn't have told him everything, if there'd been anything to tell! . . . And all the nonsense about the belt—don't you see the police here know what they're talking about? Heroin, microfilm! The woman was a mental case and probably liked the glitter. She'd nothing whatever to do with Stanley Smith."

Snatching up the belt from the table, Tessa darted away into the hotel.

A little rustle went along the terrace as people turned pages, picked up drinks and pretended that they were unaware of her passing.

Alec sat rigid, saying nothing. His lower lip was drawn in tightly under his teeth.

"Is any of that true, Alec?" Roger asked.

With a look of extreme weariness, as if he could hardly make his muscles obey him, Alec shook his head.

"No, I may have been a fool, I may have harmed her

when I—I didn't mean to. I didn't mean to, you know, but perhaps . . . It's so damned complicated. But a thing like that, a detective . . ." His lips twisted in an un-amused little grin. "I shouldn't even have known how to get hold of one."

"I could have told her so," Antonia said, "if I'd realized what she was thinking."

It was just then that the screaming started.

Just how they all knew that it was Tessa's voice scream-ing Antonia could not have said. One scream can be very like another. But the three of them came instantly to their feet and went running toward Tessa's room.

But Dave Lambrick was ahead of them. By the time Antonia reached the room, he had Tessa in his arms. She had stopped screaming and was clinging to him, hiding her face against his shoulder.

Antonia would have liked to hide her face against Roger's shoulder. But reaching the room ahead of her, he was already out on the balcony, looking out into the dusk. There was nothing for Antonia to do but to face the stare from the great black eyes of the Greek girl, Mr. Mc-Dougal's errant fiancée, who lay across the bed with the handle of a knife sticking out of her throat.

# CHAPTER ELEVEN

Separate things made unrelated impressions on Antonia's mind. She saw them all at the same time. They were all equally sharp and equally important. Or unimportant. Yes, unimportant, that was it, because the reason that she saw them in this distinct but jumbled way, like the nonsensical elements of a bad dream, was simply that they helped her not to see the central things, the body, the knife, the blood, a thin, vivid trickle of it down the girl's white throat onto the blanket.

For instance, there was Roger returning into the room from the balcony.

Suddenly he stood still. He looked at the shutters on the window. One was half closed, the other was pushed back against the wall. Apparently that meant something to him. He seemed to stand there forever, looking, frowning, immobilized.

Then there was Tessa in Dave Lambrick's arms. Perhaps it was really only a moment before she drew away from him, but a moment, after all, is not a measure of time. Some are eternal.

When she moved away, Tessa made herself look at the dead woman. Antonia wished that she would not, because the effort made her look like someone struggling violently not to be sick, and if she were sick just now, it really wouldn't help anyone in any way.

Then there was Alec, who gave Tessa one look of singular understanding, then fixed his gaze, of all things, on Antonia's belt, her gilded leather belt, the one that had come from Madame Julie, which lay half in and half out of Tessa's suitcase, together with most of Tessa's clothes, which, as usual, had never been properly unpacked.

Antonia had quite forgotten that she had left that belt in this room, but why did Alec stare at it so? Why was that important?

Then there was the poor Scottish engineer who came pushing his way through the crowd at the door, gave a chattering cry, and tried to throw himself down on the body.

Mr. Ball and Roger moved at the same time, catching him by the arms.

"Take it easy, take it easy, son," Mr. Ball said, as the young man struggled with them.

He cried out, "Let me go! She's dead—don't you see, she's dead?"

"Yes, yes, but you don't want to touch her, not just now," Mr. Ball said.

Mrs. Marinatos picked up his words. "Quite right, nobody is to touch anything! Nobody is to stay here, everybody is to go out! We send for the police."

She repeated it in Greek, in French and in German. In her excitement her shrill voice sounded more and more like a typewriter working at high speed, yet her manner was surprisingly calm. She did not start running wildly up and down as she had when the police came, wanting

135

merely to look at the passports of new arrivals.

The crowd gradually ebbed back into the passage.

"Out, please—out, please!" she cried. "*Allez, allez—hinaus!*"

Mr. Ball and Roger supported the Scotsman out. Tessa, like someone in a dream, walked out after them. Dave Lambrick stood aside so that Antonia and Alec could follow her. But Alec did not do so. He went to Tessa's suitcase and as if unthinkingly, with his mind on other things, closed it.

"Mr. Foley, please!" Mrs. Marinatos said with indignation. "You should not do that."

"Oh, sorry," Alec muttered. "I didn't like to leave it like that, everything hanging out. . . ."

From the doorway Antonia saw that although a stocking, the lace edge of a slip and the shoulder strap of a brassière were still trailing out from under the lid, the gilded belt had disappeared.

Outside the door the crowd began to resist any further orders to disperse. As more guests and waiters and chambermaids came running up to see what had happened, a solid block developed in the passage. It was hard for Roger and Mr. Ball to force a way through with the young man stumbling between them. At the end of the passage they came face to face with the sour-looking Frenchman, who would not move out of their way. Mr. Ball put a hand flat on his chest and pushed him. The Frenchman shouted at him furiously, demanding to be told what was going on. As no one answered, he elbowed his way into the crowd and began shouting his questions at the manageress.

Roger and the American steered McDougal out onto the terrace and put him down in a chair. Roger went looking for a waiter, to order whisky. Mrs. Ball appeared out of the crowd, sat down close to the young man and started talking to him in soft, comforting tones. He sat with his face in his hands, looking very much as he had when Antonia had first seen him, except that his round face, which then had been red and sweating, was now a dry, papery gray.

Seeing her looking at him, a flicker of recognition appeared in his dazed eyes. But it disappeared again. The effort of remembering where he had seen her before was beyond him.

"Now, Bob—your name's Bob, isn't it?" Mrs. Ball said. "You aren't alone here, Bob, you've got friends. Remember that. Mr. Ball and I are very, very grieved for you. We know she was a lovely person and we know how you loved her. Our hearts are sore for you, dear."

Behind Antonia, Dave Lambrick gave a desperate groan. He was in an agony of embarrassment again, as much appalled by Mrs. Ball's unself-conscious kindness as he had been a few days before by the scene of uninhibited anger made by her husband on the quay, although it was obviously the greatest luck for Bob McDougal that Mrs. Ball was there. She made him feel that in spite of their mere hour's acquaintance, she and her husband were his true friends, on whom he could count to the end. Gratefully, he let her hold one of his hands and pat it and go on murmuring kind and encouraging things to him.

Two policemen arrived within a few minutes of the telephone call made to them by Mrs. Marinatos. One was the *Astynomos*, the other was a shorter, older man with fewer white stripes on the cuff of his gray-green uniform, but with the same sort of unofficial-looking pointed shoes, rather cracked across the uppers. They went straight into the hotel, then presently the shorter one reappeared, went up to McDougal and spoke a few words to him.

McDougal only looked at him vacantly. Mr. Ball translated. They wanted him inside, he said, and offered to go with him to act as interpreter. The offer was eagerly accepted. But the policeman for some reason objected and an argument started, in which Mr. Ball's voice soon began to rise, to grow heated and every moment more Greek, at which the policeman, who had been very quiet up to that point, seemed to feel that he had the right to forget that these people were guests and to bellow too.

The two Germans and a few other spectators began to grin, then shamefacedly remembered what had caused the comic scene and did their best to suppress their amusement. Dissociating himself from the scene, Dave Lambrick walked away to the farthest end of the terrace, leaned against a vine-wreathed pillar there, and stared out wretchedly into the night.

The noise was stopped by Mr. Apodiacos, who came trotting into the hotel with a rather busy and important air, as if he were someone for whom they had all been waiting. He was fully dressed for once, in a loose gray suit and a white silk shirt and brown and white shoes, and was without his hat and sunglasses. He spoke urbanely to Mr. Ball and the policeman and calmed them down. He spoke in English to McDougal, telling him that he would act as interpreter, then took him by the arm and conducted him indoors. In passing Antonia, he bowed to her with one of his genial smiles, which, however, she no longer found as warming as she had at first. There were too many things about Mr. Apodiacos that she did not understand. For instance, the firmness with which he had just handled that scene, almost, you might say, the authority . . .

Tessa, seeing him, said, "Oh, there's that nice little man who gave us the mulberries."

It was the first thing that she had said since she had left the room where she had found the body of the murdered girl. Neither Roger nor Antonia had tried to make her talk. The three of them had sat down on a bench near the hotel entrance, while Alec had wandered away into the darkness. A very black darkness it looked from the lighted terrace, which had followed swiftly on the dusk, like a wall raised all around them to shut them in. The night was almost silent too, only one donkey at a time making an occasional sleepy effort to rouse an answer from the others, and not a transistor to be heard, and the voices from the hotel all sounding unusually hushed except now and then, when a brief clamor of excitement broke out, but died away at once, as if under a threat.

After a moment Tessa spoke again. "There was a man in there, you know."

"In there—in your room?" Roger asked.

"Yes, when I went in." She was calm, altogether too calm, like someone telling a story that had no reality for her. "I suppose he heard my key in the lock and had time to get out onto the balcony. I only had a glimpse of him as he jumped over the railing."

"Just a man, that's all you saw," Roger said. "Could it have been McDougal?"

"I didn't recognize him. He was really just a shadow. A tall man, I think. But there wasn't much light, and seeing him like that, I was scared, so I just stared instead of turning on the light at once, or running after him to see who it was. Then I did turn the light on and I saw the . . . I saw her. . . . And I started screaming, though I didn't know it until Dave rushed in."

"You'll have to tell all this to the police," Roger said.

"I know."

"Do you always keep your room locked?"

"No, I don't," she said. "I was surprised when I found it. But I assumed the maid had done it when she tidied the room. Then it took me a moment to find the key in my bag and that's how he had time to get away."

"Does the maid usually leave the door locked when she's been in?" he asked.

"I don't think so. I can't remember it happening before."

"What about the shutters outside the balcony door? Does she always fasten those?"

"Yes, she does."

"And she'd been in, hadn't she? The beds had been turned down. That'll help fix the time of the murder. I think it means too that the girl and the man you saw went into your room by the door from the corridor. They didn't come in from the balcony. I looked at how those shutters fasten. That handle you turn shoots a bolt up into the frame of the door and down into the floor. It's quite a stout affair. And there weren't any scratches or other damage that I could see."

"But why *my* room?" Tessa said. "Why did they go into *my* room?"

"A better question to ask," Roger said, "might be why did the *woman* go into your room?"

"You mean the man went in with her simply to murder her?"

"Or at least he saw her and followed her in to see what she was up to. That's why I asked if it could have been McDougal. But the man you saw may not have been the murderer. He could have seen the murderer come out of your room and gone in himself to find out what had been happening, and when he found a dead woman, then heard you at the door, lost his head and bolted." He pinched his lower lip between finger and thumb. "There are too many possibilities for convenience, aren't there?"

"But why my room?" Tessa repeated. "Why did the woman go in?"

Antonia answered, "I can think of a reason."

She had been so quiet that it seemed to surprise them both when she spoke. They turned their heads toward her.

"The other belt," she said. "She'd got the wrong belt, so she was trying again."

The blankness of Tessa's face reminded her that she had never told Tessa of her suspicion that the dead girl had been the little woman in black. She did so now, but before she finished, Roger interrupted.

"Antonia, I didn't grasp when you told me about all this that you'd actually got another *gold* belt, a belt that could have been confused with Tessa's."

"It's the one that went with the dress," she explained. "It isn't really like Tessa's at all, it's just gilded leather. I didn't like it much, so Tessa lent me hers."

"But if this girl had been told to get a gold belt that you were wearing . . ."

"Yes, that's what I meant."

"I see, I see. Where did you get this leather belt?" Roger asked.

"At Madame Julie's."

"But isn't that where you've been buying your clothes for years?"

"Yes, and it's never led to anything peculiar before. All the same, suppose this woman they've mistaken me for is another customer of Madame Julie's. Suppose that's where the confusion began."

"You mean, if she'd bought a dress like yours . . ." He paused, tugging at his lip again. "We'll think about that presently. Where's this belt now?"

"I rather think Alec's got it." Antonia told Roger how

she had left the belt in Tessa's room and forgotten it, had noticed it in the open suitcase and then seen Alec going out of his way to shut the case.

Roger swore. "If he's taken it, it complicates things, doesn't it? There's a risk of getting him into trouble for doing such a damn fool thing. Besides, if there's no belt to produce, the police aren't likely to be much interested in all this speculation."

"I'll go and look for him, shall I?" Tessa suggested.

But as she stood up she saw that Alec, who had returned without any of them noticing, was standing at the far end of the terrace, talking to Dave Lambrick. They seemed to be talking idly, only a few words at a time, merely to pass the time, yet there was a look of strain about the way they both stood.

Tessa sank down again onto the bench, her chin trembling. "Look at that!" she said. "He makes me so *furious*. . . . Questioning Dave as if . . . I'd have clutched at a tent pole in there, just to hide my eyes. Well, wouldn't anyone?"

"Meanwhile," Roger said equably, "here comes a policeman. In the circumstances, if it's any of us he wants, I think I'd say nothing about belts of any kind, unless they bring the matter up themselves."

It was the shorter of the two policemen who had just come out onto the terrace. He came up to them and intimated with gestures that Tessa should accompany him inside. Alec came quickly to her side. He said that if they wanted to question his wife, he was coming too. If the policeman did not understand the words, he understood the tone of them, nodded and turned back to the hotel. Tessa and Alec followed him.

Dave Lambrick had strolled up to Roger and Antonia behind Alec and now hovered uncertainly near them for a moment. Abruptly he pulled up a chair and sat down.

"May I ask you a question?" he said. He had a warm, pleasant voice, but he spoke with jerky haste, as if the dangers of this human contact were something to be hurried through and escaped from as fast as possible. "That girl in there, that dead girl—has she been staying in this hotel?"

"Why, have you seen her before?"

Roger returned the gaze of Dave's remarkably blue eyes with sharp interest, which made him look far more formidable than he knew. All that he intended was to give the young man his full attention, but the apparent sternness of it badly increased Dave's shyness. He nodded his head several times with a great deal of unnecessary emphasis.

"I have, I'm sure I have," he said, "but I can't recall where it was, and that worries me." With a touch of diffident defiance, as if he were confiding something which he was afraid they might not believe, he added, "I'm not all that observant."

It might have been a clumsy attempt to obtain information. On the other hand, he might have meant exactly what he had said. Antonia was inclined to believe that he had meant it.

"I don't think she was staying here," she replied. "She came in once for a drink with Mr. McDougal, but that's the only time I've seen her in the hotel. She never came into the dining room, that I know of. Perhaps you saw her somewhere up on the hill."

Dave shook his head a number of times, wrinkling his smooth, sun-tanned forehead. "No—no, I guess not. But I've seen her someplace."

"On this island or in Athens?" Roger asked.

"That's what I don't know."

"Perhaps it was on the journey," Roger suggested.

"No," Antonia said. "One of the puzzles about those two is how they got here on a day when the ship didn't call."

"The ship!" Dave Lambrick's face brightened amazingly. "That's where it was! Thanks, Mrs. Winfield. Now I'll know what to say if the cops get around to questioning me. I was worried, wondering if I should tell them I'd seen her but couldn't remember where, or if I should just say nothing about it. It isn't everyone who knows what you mean when you say you aren't observant."

"Both of us," Antonia said reassuringly, "happen to be quite accustomed to people whose minds are elsewhere."

"That's what I thought." He gave her a grateful smile.

"Only you can't have seen the girl on the ship," Antonia said. "I'm quite sure she wasn't there."

"She was." He was as positive now as he had been hesitant before. "She and the guy who was with her got out of a car and went straight on board just as the bus I was in got there. We were the last out of the bus station and last onto the ferryboat, so we were the first off and the first to get to the quay, and I was one of the first off the bus and onto the ship after them. And they were walking up and down the deck together, watching the buses arrive and arguing, because the girl was saying she always got seasick and wanted to go below and the guy was saying she couldn't get sick on a day like that and she'd be better off on deck. After that I didn't see them again, so I reckon they went below."

"I didn't see the car on the ferryboat," Antonia argued.

"Maybe it came over on an earlier ferry," Dave said.

Roger nodded. "And then the two of them came off the ship after everyone else."

"I didn't notice that," Dave said, beginning to look uncomfortable. "I was thinking about something else."

Antonia knew what he had been thinking about. He had

been thinking about the noise and the fuss made by Mr. Ball over having his luggage weighed, and the dreadfulness of being of the same nationality as someone who didn't mind making a spectacle of himself for such a paltry reason.

But had it been a paltry reason?

She gave a startled shiver. How suspicious of other people could you let yourself become without going mad? Yet wasn't it possible that Mr. Ball had had a very good reason for making that scene on the quay? For certainly, once the scene had started, no one there had paid any attention to anything else. It would have been the easiest thing in the world for two people to come ashore and go quietly away out of sight without being noticed.

But suspicion, once started, didn't stop there. For now Antonia remembered Mrs. Ball chatting with Bob McDougal before the murder, listening to him, cheering and advising him, and of course, keeping him sitting there for as long as she could while the girl went about her mysterious business. . . .

Antonia turned her head, meaning to take a thoughtful look at the Balls, but instead found herself staring with horror at a tall, thin figure in shorts and a checked shirt that had just emerged from the darkness, reached the edge of the terrace, and stood still there, grasping one of the pillars and blinking as if the lights dazzled him. It was Stanley Smith. With the light shining down on him from over his head, his face looked unnaturally pale, with holes of shadow carved into it. The front of his shirt was covered in dark red stains. He was clasping a shapeless black bundle.

# CHAPTER TWELVE

He saw Antonia and came straight toward her. Although his chest was far redder than that of the dead girl, he did not stagger or collapse. There was an excited smile on his face.

He dumped his bundle on Antonia's lap.

"There's your little woman in black, Mrs. Winfield."

It was damp and a lot of sand fell out of it. The wet black stuff felt to Antonia as if it had life of its own and would wind clinging tentacles around her and smother her. She pushed it violently away and pointed a shaking finger at his chest. "You're hurt. . . ."

"Oh, that," he said. "One of the Apodiacos kids spilt a basin of mulberries over me. Makes me look as if someone had made a start at flaying me alive, doesn't it?"

Roger picked up the bundle and spread it out.

"You're Mr. Smith?" he said. "Mr. Smith, would you care to elaborate on what you meant by calling this a woman, little or large, which it most undeniably is not?"

The unusual pomposity of Roger's manner told Antonia that he was working hard to cover up some feeling about

Stanley Smith, but her own attention was still riveted on his stained shirt. Because of what it reminded her of, the sight made her feel sick, yet she could not look away.

"I just meant it's what she wore," he answered. "The little woman who stole Mrs. Winfield's belt. You've heard all about that, I imagine."

"And about you too and your previous encounters with my wife."

"A mistake of some sort," Smith said casually. "I probably look like a dozen other people."

"Probably," Roger agreed. "Now about this garment..." Spread out, it obviously was a garment of sorts, a sacklike thing with flapping sleeves and a round hole for a neck. "May I ask how and where you discovered it?"

"I found it just beyond the windmill, half buried in the sand," Smith said.

"You were looking for it?"

For the first time Smith appeared to give Roger his full attention. They studied one another, each measuring some quality in the other. Then, rather to Antonia's surprise, both smiled. The smiles were cautious, but there was an odd look of recognition in them.

"No," Stanley Smith said. "Why should I be?"

"What do I know about the motivations of your actions?" Roger asked.

Smith's smile broadened, as if he found this a very subtly humorous remark. "Well, I was just walking along and I found it by chance," he said.

"In the dark? You saw this black thing half-buried in the sand in the dark?"

"It isn't so very dark, once you're used to it."

It was at that moment that Antonia reached out and dabbed with her handkerchief at a red clot on Stanley Smith's chest. He shied away at her touch, then as she looked at the portion of squashed mulberry that had come away on the handkerchief, he shook his head at her.

"I told you it wasn't blood, Mrs. Winfield," he said. "You've altogether too much imagination."

She shuddered and did not answer.

Roger said, "There's some reason for us both to have blood on our minds, but perhaps you know that, even if you've been out walking in the dark."

Smith gave no sign of having heard. He began to gather up the black bundle.

"I'd better take this thing along to the police," he said. "I brought it here first because I thought Mrs. Winfield would be glad to know where her little woman went to."

"And where *did* she go to?" Roger asked.

"Into a hole in the sand. The black part of her. The rest —this is my reading of it—simply went into the sea and swam away. Don't ask me why. Your guess is as good as mine."

"Not quite, perhaps, but nearly."

Again Antonia had that disturbing feeling that perfect understanding existed between Roger and Stanley Smith.

"But I don't believe Mrs. Winfield is much interested," Smith said. "I might just as well have gone to the police straightaway."

"Having gone first, however, to see Mr. Apodiacos," Roger said.

Smith paused in rolling up the bundle. His hands became still. Seeing some of those macabre mulberry stains on them as well as on his chest, Antonia wished that he would hurry up and go away and wash.

"One passes the house, you know," he said, "on the way back from the mill, and the kids were in the garden."

"I see," Roger said.

Smith gave a brief chuckle. "Be careful, professor. Detection can grow to be quite a vice."

"You've some experience of it?"

"As I told Mrs. Winfield, I've experience of a lot of things."

"Well, you'll find both Mr. Apodiacos and the police in the hotel, which will save you some trouble."

"Thanks." Smith appeared to take the information as a matter of course. He tucked the bundle under his arm and walked off.

When he had gone Roger reached for one of Antonia's hands and held it, as if he felt that she needed to be given reassurance.

She sighed and said, "Roger, I believe you *liked* him."

"Is that how it looked? I hadn't even thought about it," he answered. "I was just thinking you're probably about to find out a good deal about that young man."

"I hope so. It ought to be interesting."

Dave Lambrick stood up. He stretched and yawned.

"Are they going to give us any dinner tonight, or do we go hungry?" he said. "I think I'll go and see." But he went on standing there instead of leaving them, and after a moment brought out another of his hurried, urgent statements. "I guess you thought he'd heard about the murder."

"I shouldn't be surprised," Roger said.

"Did he hear it from those kids he mentioned, or was he in the hotel when it happened, but not letting on?"

"As he would say, your guess is as good as mine."

Dave gave a slight shake of his head, as if he did not feel inclined to claim as much insight into the situation as Roger possessed.

As he walked off Antonia screwed her reddened handkerchief into a ball and deposited it in an ashtray. She felt as much distaste for it as she would have if the stains had been blood.

"Explain what you meant," she said, "about Stanley Smith going to Mr. Apodiacos first."

"Well, wasn't it a curious thing to do?"

"But it's true that he'd have to pass the house coming back, just as he said, and the children really might have stopped him."

"Then perhaps I'm wrong. But think of what he told us. He was out for a walk along the beach and he stumbled across that black thing, half-buried in sand, and in spite of the darkness, he knew at once what it was and what it meant and he took it straight to Mr. Apodiacos. And it happens that the first thing the police seem to have done, when they heard of the murder, was to send for Mr. Apodiacos. And as soon as he got here, it looked to me very much as if he were simply taking charge."

"So really you think that he and Stanley Smith . . ."

Antonia had no chance to finish what was in her mind about them because the shorter policeman appeared just then and signaled to her and Roger to go with him.

He took them into the manageress' private office. Passing through the entrance hall to reach it, they saw Tessa and Alec standing near the door that led out onto the beach. Tessa made a signal to them that Antonia did not understand, then the two of them went out into the darkness together.

There seemed to be a great many people standing about, more than Antonia had realized the hotel contained. The dining room door was closed, although the hour for dinner was long past, and two waiters lounged near it, keeping out the hungry.

Like the hall, Mrs. Marinatos' office had far more people in it than it was meant to contain, and although the windows were open, there did not seem to be enough air to go around. The pleasant, flower-scented warmth of the evening became a choking blast of heat that smelled of cigar smoke and people.

Mr. Apodiacos was smoking the cigar. He apologized for it, asked Antonia if she minded, offered a cigar to Roger and ordered the policeman who had fetched them to place chairs for them both. The *Astynomos* sat at a big desk, looking full of authority but saying nothing. In a corner of the room sat the Italian with the heavily veined face and mop of curly gray hair whom Stanley Smith had brought back from the harbor that morning. Stanley Smith himself was leaning against a windowsill, looking quite at ease in this company. He had washed off most of the mulberry juice and put on a clean shirt. He had a cigarette between his long fingers. The black bundle that he had brought in was on the desk in front of the *Astynomos*.

Roger addressed him with a half smile. "So you *are* one of them."

Stanley Smith grinned faintly back. "I thought you'd caught on. Yes, but only private and not much good at that, evidently, since Mrs. Winfield spotted me the first day I started following her. I don't know what I did wrong, but she only needed one look at me to know what I was there for."

"You had bad luck," Roger said. "You happened to remind her very strongly of someone she knew. But no doubt her acuteness greatly increased your unsuspiciousness of her."

"Well, naturally, it did," Smith agreed. "There was quite a touch of professionalism about it."

"I hope you're going to tell us *what* profession you

thought she belonged to," Roger said. "I take it for granted, of course, that you've realized you were mistaken."

"Please, please!" Mr. Apodiacos broke in. "All these are very important questions and we will return to them, but first my friend here has questions he must ask you." He turned to the man seated at the desk and they spoke rapidly together for a moment. Then Mr. Apodiacos went on. "He wishes to know, please, where you and Mrs. Winfield were this evening, let us say from five o'clock onwards."

"Why five o'clock?" Roger asked. "The girl was killed much later than that, wasn't she?"

"Yes, perhaps only five, ten minutes before Mrs. Foley found her and that was nearly seven o'clock. We shall know more of that presently. She was killed by being stabbed in the throat. But my friend here believes she may have been unconscious when it happened. I think perhaps he is right. Otherwise there are some things about her death I cannot explain. For instance, why did she not scream? Everyone heard Mrs. Foley when she screamed, so why did this girl not scream to save her life?"

"You mean someone knocked her out, then cold-bloodedly stabbed her?" Roger said.

"Maybe. We come back to that later. Now please if you will be so good as to answer my friend's questions."

Roger told them how he and Antonia had spent the afternoon. Then Antonia was asked when she had first seen the dead girl. She described their meeting in the hotel in Athens.

She was asked how often she had seen the girl since then.

"Twice," she answered. "I think it was twice. But we didn't speak to each other either time."

"Where did you see her these two times?" Mr. Apodiacos asked.

"Once here in the hotel," she said. "It was the day before yesterday. She and Mr. McDougal came in for a drink before dinner. The other time . . . You know when the other time was, Mr. Apodiacos?"

"Mrs. Winfield, you always think I know so much more than I do." He lifted his hands toward her with the palms turned outward, a gesture to show that he was concealing nothing. "I am not a man of great knowledge."

"Well, I think—I'm sure—she was the woman in black who followed me into the mill and stole my belt."

"And why are you sure of that?"

She made a gesture similar to his.

"Aha!" he said. "Intuition!"

"A little more than that," she said defensively. "I—well, I recognized her. She had very unusual eyes."

"And she went into Mrs. Foley's room for some reason, didn't she?" Roger said. "Wasn't it probably to look for what she had failed to find when she attacked my wife?"

"If I knew what she was looking for, I could perhaps say if it was probable or not," Mr. Apodiacos said.

"I'm sure you know a great deal more about it than we do," Antonia said.

"There again, you are so sure of so much. I am sure of nothing, Mrs. Winfield, nothing."

"Then ask Mr. Smith!" she said in a louder, challenging tone.

Smith knocked cigarette ash out of the window. "As a matter of fact," he said, "I agree with Mrs. Winfield. I'd already worked out that the woman literally couldn't have walked away from the mill without being seen by a number of people, including, as it happened, Mr. Apodiacos himself, whose word I was prepared to accept. Therefore, she'd never left the mill. Not in the form Mrs. Winfield described. But if she'd been in a swimsuit when she slipped out of the door, with the black dress rolled up in a towel, and if she'd dumped the things there and gone straight into the sea, she might easily have got away without being noticed. So I asked those two Germans if they'd seen a girl swimming near them, though I don't think it's in their nature to notice a girl. However, they thought they had. So this evening I went looking around and found that thing there. . . ." He nodded at the bundle on the table. "But the trouble for the girl was, the thing she'd stolen from Mrs. Winfield wasn't the thing she wanted. So later she went into Mrs. Foley's room to look for it. I imagine she'd already searched Mrs. Winfield's room. Mrs. Winfield was away for most of the afternoon. There'd been plenty of opportunity."

Antonia leaned forward, looking at him hard. *"But what was she looking for?"*

"Please!" Mr. Apodiacos said again. "Let us take everything in order. Let us say for the present you are right, it was this girl who has been murdered who stole Mrs. Foley's belt from you. And you had seen her once in Athens. Good. Now did you not see her on your journey here, for she arrived the same day as you?"

"No, but Mr. Lambrick can tell you about that," Antonia said. "She seems to have been deliberately keeping out of sight."

"And that is all you know about her? That is almost as little as her fiancée knows. He knows her name, or what she chose to say was her name, and nothing else. Not surprising, if what he tells us is true, that they met for the first time a week ago, and he spent most of that week, he has explained, in a state of intoxication. They arrived on the same ship as yourselves and have been staying in a house upstairs." He waved a hand in the direction of the hilltop. "He says it was her choice that they should come here, for the sake of peace and quiet. Peace and quiet! I tell you, anyone who says to me, 'I look for peace and quiet,' I do not trust."

"But why?" Antonia said plaintively. "Really, Mr. Apodiacos, I think you're quite irrational on that point. Peace and quiet are absolutely all that I want at the moment."

"And what do you find, eh?" he asked with a flash of ferocity. "Do you find them?"

"That has nothing to do with it."

"Are you sure? Are you sure you do not find what you seek?"

"More and more sure every minute."

"You are sure of so many things," he said with a shake of his head. "I tell you again, I am sure of nothing." He pondered this state of affairs, puffing at his cigar. "Please, Mrs. Winfield, is there anyone in this hotel you have ever seen before you came here?"

"Mr. Smith," Antonia answered promptly.

"Yes, yes, but apart from him—and, of course, Mr. Mc-Dougal."

"No, nobody."

"And you came here yourself only for peace and quiet —you still say that?"

"I do, I do!"

"Mr. Apodiacos," Roger said, "I really believe you might find it helpful if you were to take us a little more into your confidence. If you were to suggest to Mr. Smith, for instance, that he should tell us why he's been following my wife. Her own belief is that he's mistaken her for somebody else. Well, mightn't you save yourselves a lot of trouble by straightening that out?"

"We might indeed, if it were true," Mr. Apodiacos replied, "but as it happens, my friends Mr. Smith and Mr. Murillo"—he gestured at Stanley Smith and the curly-haired Italian—"do not make such mistakes. Mrs. Winfield's activities have been under observation for a number of years—"

"*Years?*" Roger and Antonia said together, and Roger went on, "What the hell are you talking about?"

Mr. Apodiacos gave a sigh. "I think it is more than likely you know nothing of what she has done. It is a matter over which ladies have very little conscience and husbands are often kept in the dark. But now, you see, it has led to murder. Oh, I do not think she intended it, or ever considered the dangerous character of the people with whom she was associating—"

"Now wait a moment!" Roger roared out in a voice he had almost never used in his life except when he had found himself, most unwillingly, lecturing to first-year medical students. He leaped to his feet, his lean body taut with outrage. "Now wait—!"

He stopped himself and drew a long breath. He looked as if he were counting ten.

"Let's take this calmly," he said with a deliberately lowered voice. "Let's go into it carefully. You believe that without my knowledge my wife has been engaged in some sort of illegal activity—for years. You believe—" In spite of himself, his voice was rising again. "Good God, man, it's completely fantastic! Of course you've got her mixed up with someone else. That character—" He pointed a rigid finger at Stanley Smith. "That friend of yours who has just admitted to us all his inefficiency as a detective—"

Smith interrupted, "You said yourself that was just my bad luck."

"Mere politeness," Roger snarled back. "Your inefficiency as a detective is beyond question, since my normally quite unsuspicious wife realized at once that you were following her, and since you were also seen by a number of our neighbors, hanging about near our house, and since you were almost caught in the act of burgling it by one of our policemen. Your incapacity is proved beyond all doubt. So you can hardly be regarded as a reliable source of information. It amazes me that any responsible person should listen to you. I doubt if I'd believe you myself if you told me what time of day it was. The chances are it would turn out that you'd forgotten to wind your watch for the last three days."

"Look," Smith said placatingly, "I don't know anything about a burglary."

"You were seen there," Roger told him.

"Not in your house or breaking into it," Smith said. "When did it happen?"

"The night my wife left for Greece."

"How long after she left?"

"Some hours."

"In that case it's going to be quite easy to prove, if I have to, that I was nowhere near your house any longer. My job was to follow Mrs. Winfield. I knew I'd made a mess of it in the afternoon so I'd phoned up from Farr's and told them that she'd spotted me, but I'd been told to get after her again and not worry if she saw me. It would make her nervous and might make her do something stupid. But when I saw her leave in the taxi, I went to the nearest telephone and asked for more instructions. We weren't prepared for her to go off like that. We knew she hated flying. We knew she always went by train. When the news of the railway strike in France came through we thought she'd probably put off the whole thing and go a bit later. It wasn't as if she'd a job with only a short holiday that couldn't be changed. What we hadn't allowed for was the influence of Mrs. Foley."

"Then why were you hanging round the house, if you thought she wouldn't leave?" Roger asked.

"To be on the safe side. Also to watch out for the other people if they turned up. It was as important for them as for us to know what she was going to do in view of the strike. But they left it a bit too long. That's what I make of your story of the burglary. They broke in, meaning to recover the stuff, but she'd gone already. That's why they contacted the girl in Athens and put her on the job of trailing Mrs. Winfield."

While he talked, Antonia had started to shiver. It seemed impossible that anyone could feel cold in that stifling little room, but a chill like the chill of fever had entered her blood. For this man and those other people of whom he had spoken, whoever they were, had not mistaken her for anybody else. They knew too much about her for that. They knew of her dislike of flying, they knew that she liked to travel by train, they knew almost as much about her as any fairly close friend.

"These other people," Roger said, "who are they?"

Stanley Smith shrugged his shoulders. "Ask your wife, professor. And if by any chance she doesn't know . . ." He glanced at her and she was momentarily surprised by the sympathy in his expression. "I mean, if she's an entirely innocent tool, then the less you all know, the better for you. You see, something's gone badly wrong for those people. The girl was given the job of following you and getting hold of this thing Mrs. Winfield had, but when she went searching for it in Mrs. Foley's room someone else got in too, killed her and got away with the loot. So we're dealing with two criminals who are up against each other. And you don't want to be caught between them if there's any more murdering to be done. Anyway, my instructions were to tell you no more than I had to."

"But they didn't—" Abruptly Antonia stopped herself. She had nearly said that the murderer had not got away with the loot. It was Alec who had done that. It was he who had taken the gold leather belt from Tessa's suitcase and disappeared with it into the darkness.

# CHAPTER THIRTEEN

Eying Stanley Smith thoughtfully, Mr. Apodi-
acos said, "I believe greatly in frankness myself. I do not
like unnecessary concealment."

This struck Antonia as most unlikely to be true, but she
hoped that, perhaps for some reason of his own, the Greek
wanted to take her and Roger a little into his confidence.

He went on, "I must talk this over with my friend
Smith." The pretense that there was any need for him to
talk anything over with the *Astynomos*, however important he looked seated at the desk, had been wholly
abandoned. "Perhaps I shall persuade him his instructions
are not sensible. I like always to act as I think best and not
as anyone tells me. I am individualist."

He went on to thank Antonia and Roger in a stately,
carefully memorized phrase for helping the police in their
inquiries. As they rose to go he gave a dimpling smile and
bowed, the bow making him wince a little as his belt
chafed the peeling patch of sunburn hidden by his shirt.

The dining room was open now and dinner was being
served. Roger and Antonia went to their table. The room

was unnaturally quiet. When people wanted to talk to one another, they leaned across the tables and whispered.

"I don't really want to eat anything at all," Antonia said, looking blankly at the menu handed to her by the waiter and wondering where Tessa and Alec had got to.

"Better have a try," Roger said. "I think I'll have lobster —no, I'll start with soup, then I'll have lobster, then grilled steak, potatoes, salad. . . . And we want some wine, of course. What was that rosé we had at lunch?"

In a crisis Roger always felt that it was necessary to keep up his strength. Luckily, although crises in the academic world are frequent, this had never led him to put on a pound of extra weight.

"Soup and an omelet, please," Antonia said, and as soon as the waiter left them wished that she had asked for the soup only. She put her elbows on the table and took her head in her hands. "Roger, were we right to say nothing about the belt—the one that belonged to the dress?"

"How could we say anything when we don't know why Alec took it or what he's done with it?" Roger said. "I suppose there's no question he did take it?"

"I didn't actually see him take it," she answered. "I just saw him shutting the case."

"Could anyone else have taken it? There were several other people in the room, Ball, Lambrick, McDougal, a few others."

"Alec was the nearest to the case," she said, "and he did shut it."

There was a short silence, then Roger observed thoughtfully, "That Frenchman made an awful fuss about something in the passage."

"But he couldn't have taken the belt, or killed the girl. He was out on the terrace all the time we were there." Convinced that she had no desire at all for food, Antonia was astonished all of a sudden to realize that she was voraciously eating dry bread. She put it down on her plate and pushed it away from her. Almost at once her nervous fingers reached for it again. "I was wrong, wasn't I?" she said. "They haven't mistaken me for somebody else. They know too much about me."

"Looks like it," Roger agreed.

"They've made some incredible mistake about me, but it isn't that."

"Don't look so miserable," he said. "We'll get out of this somehow and we'll ditch Tessa and Alec and we'll go and have a really good holiday together where there's some genuine peace and quiet."

" 'There's no peace for the wicked. . . .' " She had a feeling that she was going to break down and start crying in public. "But what have I done? I'm not wicked! I'm not criminal! I only wanted to have a nice holiday, and I planned everything so carefully and put lots of thought into it and I was absolutely sure nothing could go wrong."

"Possibly that's been the whole trouble," Roger said. "Let's think this out. You always plan every holiday carefully, don't you? You always go at the same time of year and do practically the same as you did the year before, and you like to discuss all the details with as many people as possible, so a lot of people know exactly what you're going to do, and how and when."

"I really do all that?" she said. "Am I really such a bore about it?"

"Well, isn't it a fact that when you start to plan a holiday the first thing you do is to go to Farr's and talk to some man there who's been looking after you for years, and get him to fix things up? Then a bit later you begin to think of new clothes and you go along to Madame What's-her-name and buy a thing or two. And . . ." He paused, thinking. "Yes, as I remember it, you generally have some alterations done, don't you? You've often complained you aren't a stock size. And then you collect your tickets and your new clothes and in a day or two off you go by train—by train and sleeper—to somewhere in the south. Isn't that right?"

She was looking at him in amazement. "Imagine you noticing all that! I hardly knew it myself. Yes, it's absolutely right."

"It's happened often enough for me to have become aware of a certain pattern in your proceedings," Roger replied.

"Still, what difference does it make? Why is it important?"

"Well . . ." Roger tasted the chicken soup flavored with lemon which the waiter had just brought to them and decided that he liked it. "What about this for a possibility? You go to Madame Julie. You choose a dress. The dress has, say, a belt that's a bit on the solid side—"

"Yes," Antonia interrupted, "one of the reasons I like her things is that the belts and buttons and so on don't look cheap and ordinary. They're made of good material and the design's interesting. She's told me they're specially made for her by a small firm in Paris."

"Exactly. Well, you choose the dress and you leave it with her for alterations to be made. And one of the alterations she makes is with the buckle of the belt. Did this belt of yours have a large buckle?"

"Yes, too large, with some colored stones in it. It was altogether too much of a good thing. That's why I found I didn't like it."

163

"Suppose it's a trick buckle, then, has a spring some-where, opens. . . . She fills it up with—something—we don't know what. Then you collect the dress and you very innocently set off with it, crossing several frontiers, where a tourist like you almost never has her baggage thoroughly examined. And at some point on the journey, while you're in the dining car and the *wagon-lit* attendant has his at-tention distracted, someone slips into your sleeper, opens your suitcase, which you probably haven't even left locked, opens the trick buckle, takes out whatever's inside it and quietly departs."

Antonia found that she had been holding her breath. She let it out slowly.

"But Madame Julie's such a nice person," she said. "I've always liked her. She takes such trouble over things, even quite cheap things, and she takes such an interest. . . . Yes, I see, go on. What happens next?"

"Nothing, so far as you're concerned, until next year, when it happens all over again."

"So all this time I've been a smuggler without knowing it?"

"I believe a lot of smuggling's done that way," Roger said. "The most successful smugglers are the ones who don't know what they're carrying. However, someone found out about it, and Stanley Smith was given the job of following you."

"I rather wish they'd arrested me on the spot," Antonia said. "Why didn't they?"

"Partly, perhaps, because they didn't know how much you knew about what you were doing. Apodiacos was quite right, lots of otherwise respectable people have very little conscience about smuggling. But I imagine their real concern was to see who popped into your sleeper or made a contact with you on the train. It would be much more important to get that person than you."

"Then all their plans were upset by the railway strike in France."

"And Tessa."

"Yes, if Tessa hadn't arrived that evening, I'd simply have stayed at home."

"And the burglar would have retrieved the belt and that would have been the last you'd have known about it for this summer. As it was, Smith and that Italian and the girl all had to come chasing after you all the way here."

"And the murderer," Antonia said. "He may be one of them or someone quite different."

A shadow fell across their table. Someone had come up behind Antonia. It made her start as if a hand had been suddenly laid on her shoulder.

"Mind if I join you folks?" Mr. Ball said. "Mrs. Ball's still looking after that poor guy McDougal. He's taking it hard. I've had some food sent to them and now somehow I don't fancy eating by myself. Not tonight, though I've seen violence in my time and I guess these islands have too." He dropped wearily into a chair.

"This isn't the way Mrs. Ball and I planned to spend our week here," he said. "A rest was what we wanted. We've been to Rhodes and Crete and Mikonos and Delphi and Nauplion and Sounion and Corinth and Marathon and Mycenae and—oh, every place you ever heard of, and we've gone sore-footed in the heat over more stony ground and listened to more lectures per square foot of ruin than I thought the human frame could stand. Athens, too— did I forget to say Athens? Yes, well, we saw Athens from end to end. And when we leave here we fly to Rome and make a start on Italy. So you can see how a rest would seem a good idea. A rest . . . ! Another few days of this kind of rest will just about kill me."

"Then you're leaving on the next boat?" Antonia said.

"The very next! If there was one tomorrow we'd leave on that. Well, I can't speak for Mrs. Ball, but it's what I'd do myself. Mrs. Ball would never leave Bob McDougal if she felt he was depending on her. That's the trouble about traveling with Mrs. Ball. She can spot a lame duck with just one glance, then she can't rest till she's helped sort out his problems for him. My problem's going to be when the supply of lame ducks runs out. I've spent thirty years worrying she'd end by going to work on me." He gave an abrupt laugh. "Pardon the crap I'm talking. It's just that I can't get that picture out of my mind. That girl, the knife . . . Shall I tell you something?"

He picked up a fork and began idly to draw a pattern on the tablecloth.

"I've seen something of the world," he said, "and I don't mean going on tours and listening to lectures. And the first time I saw that girl, I said to myself, 'She's trouble.' And when I saw McDougal and the way he was drinking, I wanted to say to him, 'Son, you'll be drinking something a lot stronger than Scotch one day, like sulphuric acid, if you stick around with her, or perhaps it'll be a knife between your ribs. . . .'" He gave a dubious smile. "Maybe that sounds as if I'm trying to be wise after the event. What I mean is, if the knife that killed the girl was her own, it wouldn't surprise me. If the guy who went in there with her and killed her didn't plan to do it. If it was she who started it. If it was a kind of self-defense."

"It sounds rather as if you think McDougal did it," Roger said.

"Maybe he did. If so, I'm not sure I'd blame him. Only the police seem to think she was knocked unconscious first and then deliberately stabbed. You see, she didn't scream. Yet she was stabbed from in front, so she would have seen it coming."

Mr. Ball dropped the fork with a clatter, as if it had failed to prove his point.

"All the same," he said, "could be I'm right that she had the knife and drew it on whoever was with her and he knocked her out and then decided he'd better finish the job."

Tessa and Alec came in just then, but because Mr. Ball was at the table, it was impossible to ask Alec if he had taken the golden leather belt from Tessa's room and what he had done with it. They talked of all the sights that the Balls had seen on other islands and the mainland. The meal passed slowly. The pauses between the courses were longer than usual and from time to time there were sounds of excitement in the kitchen, hurriedly quelled by the staccato voice of Mrs. Marinatos.

A little while before the meal ended the shorter policeman came in and asked Mr. Ball to go with him. He stood up, smiled around the table and thanked them all for their company. As he walked heavily away, a look of truculence developed in the set of his shoulders and the way he planted his feet, an air of being ready to stand up for himself whatever happened.

When he had gone Roger said, low-voiced, "Well, where is it, Alec?"

Alec tapped his pocket.

"What made you take it?" Roger asked.

"It seemed the obvious thing to do at the time," Alec answered. "But it appears to be a perfectly normal belt."

"Have you taken it apart?"

"Not yet."

"Then suppose we go upstairs and do a thorough job on

it now," Roger said. "By the way, where are you going to sleep tonight? Have you arranged anything about that?"

"Mrs. Marinatos has given us a room near yours," Tessa said. "It's at the back and it hasn't got a balcony, but it'll do. She said that as soon as the police allow it, she'll have our luggage moved up there."

Antonia gave Roger a worried look. "If you do take that belt apart, won't it be tampering with evidence?"

"The very word for it," he said. "Come along, let's go and tamper."

"You'd never do it if you were at home," she said. "You'd have too much respect for the law."

"I think that would rather depend on how much respect the law seemed to have for me," he said. "If Smith had shown a little more trust in our good sense and civic virtues and had told us more of what all the skullduggery is about, I might feel more inclined to hand over the evidence unexamined. As it is, it's pure surmise that that belt is evidence of anything of the least importance. So if you, as its owner, feel like cutting it into little bits, I don't see why you shouldn't."

"Smith? Stanley Smith?" Tessa said, looking quickly from Roger to Antonia. "Where does he come in?"

"A detective, my dear," Antonia said. "A dear little private detective."

"Come along," Roger said again, standing up. "We'll tell you all about it upstairs."

In their bedroom Roger went straight to the window and threw the shutters back.

"You'll have every insect within miles making straight for our light if you do that," Antonia warned him.

He went out onto the balcony, returned and closed the shutters again.

"I just wanted to make sure we were alone," he said. "Now let's have that belt, Alec."

"Tell us about Smith first," Tessa said. "I want to understand what's been happening."

Briefly Antonia told her what she and Roger had learned about Stanley Smith that evening. While she was speaking, Alec brought the rolled-up belt out of his pocket and gave it to Roger, who ran it through his fingers, holding it close to the light. He turned it this way and that, feeling its thickness and examining the construction of the buckle. The buckle held him longest, then suddenly he held the belt out to Antonia.

"Put it on," he said. "Let's see how it looks."

She took it and fastened it around her waist.

"Oh dear, I believe I've been putting on weight," she muttered as she fumbled for the right hole. She looked at herself in the mirror. "It's really rather awful, isn't it? I don't know why I ever thought I liked it. Of course, it doesn't belong to this dress, but still . . ." She undid the buckle again and handed the belt back to Roger.

He took a penknife out of his pocket.

"If there's a trick to the buckle, as I imagine there must be, I can't find it," he said, "so I'm going to slit the belt up and somehow bust the buckle open. Any objections?"

"Go ahead," she said.

Sitting down on the edge of the bed, he went to work. He began on the stitching that held the leather and the lining together. He went at it slowly, with precision and delicacy. He would not be hurried. The others stood around him, stooping to see what he was doing, except when he complained that they were getting in the light. Antonia became so impatient that she wanted to snatch the penknife from him and rip and slash until the leather was in ribbons.

Roger cut through the stitching all along one side of the belt, then gently poked the blade of the knife in between the leather and the lining. They were lightly stuck together with some gluey substance, but came apart quite easily as he worked the knife along between them. Carefully he separated the two strips of material from end to end of the belt.

"Nothing," Alec said, peering over Roger's shoulder.

"Not a damn thing," Roger agreed without any sound of disappointment. "I didn't really expect it."

He started work on the eyelets that fastened the leather to the buckle. He dug them out, pulled the leather away and dropped it onto the coverlet beside him. Then again he began turning the big ornate buckle around in his fingers, looking for a point where he could jab in the tip of the knife.

"Try stamping on it," Antonia suggested.

"Not when we don't know what's inside it," he said. "If it's something that might spill . . . Ah!" He had just managed to work loose one of the colored stones set in the gilded metal. In another moment he had the stone out. Soon he had dug out two more and after that found that he was able to dig the knife into the thin metal behind. The buckle split and bent. It was of a cheap-looking, lead-colored metal and solid. There was no possibility that there had ever been anything inside it.

Roger tossed it down on the bed together with his knife. He stood up.

"All wrong," he said. "Wrong from beginning to end. It can't have been what they were after. Have to think again."

He went to the shutters, pushed them open, stepped out onto the balcony, gripped the iron railing before him and gazed out into the night.

# CHAPTER FOURTEEN

Alec seemed about to follow Roger out, then he changed his mind and turned to Antonia.

"I expect you're both very tired," he said. "You'd like us to go. Come along, Tessa. Goodnight, Mrs. Winfield. Goodnight, professor."

He spoke in that formally considerate tone which was the nearest that he ever came to sounding friendly to Tessa's relations.

"Goodnight, my dears," Antonia answered absently, her eyes on Roger.

Tessa bent over her and kissed her, then went out with Alec. They began to talk softly to one another before the door was quite closed, and for some reason that made them seem so like any happily married couple with comfortably established habits of feeling and acting together that momentarily Antonia's knowledge that the marriage had broken up was blotted out. Her memory of it returned with a bewildering little shock. She walked out onto the balcony and stood beside Roger.

"What do you really think is the matter with Alec?" she asked. "Why doesn't he like us?"

"Doesn't he?" Roger said. "I always thought he was rather particularly attached to you."

"To me?" she said in surprise. "I'm sure he isn't."

"Afraid of showing it, perhaps. His own family don't seem to have gone in for that much. A rather miserable lot, I thought, going on the little I've seen of them."

"I've always felt he was basically hostile to both of us," she said.

"Oh, I don't think so."

"I don't think you ever think so. You've a deplorable way of noticing the best in other people and thinking it's all there is. Look at how you took to that man Smith."

"You're still against him, are you?" Roger put an arm around her shoulders. "He was just doing his job."

"Remember he's kept me in a state of panic for days," she said as she leaned against him. "He's got an awful lot to live down. And the way that he won't tell us even now what it's all about, I don't like that. What *is* it all about, anyway? What can it be about if we've been quite wrong about the belt?"

Roger did not answer. They stood in silence, side by side, with the light breeze from the sea on their faces. The waves murmured softly below them, invisible except for the pale edging of foam. The sky was full of stars.

After a little while Roger observed, "You know, it's really very pleasant here. I've been missing something, haven't I?"

"That's what I always thought," she said, "but perhaps there's something I miss in fishing."

"Suppose we come here together another year, when conditions are more normal . . ."

There was a sound behind them. They both turned.

Neither Antonia nor Roger had heard the door of their bedroom open or close, but it must have done so after they had gone out onto the balcony, for a man was standing in the middle of the room, quietly listening to them. It was the dyspeptic-looking Frenchman who had arrived that day. He had a gun in his hand. He said in a harsh whisper, "Silence! Keep quiet and do what I tell you. Stand over there."

He pointed to a corner of the room. His yellow face wore exactly the same expression as it had when he had been contemplating the results of Greek cookery. The job on which he was engaged evidently held no attractions for him but, like the food that he despised, was necessary to his continued existence.

Neither Roger nor Antonia stirred. She could not have done so just then. Her muscles were frozen.

"Quick!" the Frenchman said in the same throaty whisper. "Faces to the wall."

"But you can't do any shooting here," Roger said. "Too noisy."

"I will shoot if I must."

"You wouldn't even get downstairs."

"A man with a gun can go where he likes until he meets another man with a gun." He pointed peremptorily at the corner. "Over there!"

They crossed to the corner and stood facing the wall.

"Now where is it?" he demanded.

"Where is what?" Roger asked.

"The belt, the belt!"

"On the bed, what's left of it."

"Not that, the other one."

"The other—?" Roger bit the sentence off.

"Where is it?" the Frenchman asked impatiently.

Antonia heard him come a step nearer to them. As he

did so, the pale blue wall in front of her seemed to recede into the misty distance. A mosquito landed elegantly on it a few inches from her face. She stared at it, focusing with all her will on its small, delicate viciousness.

"We don't know," Roger said. "We haven't got it."

"Where is it? I have no time to waste."

"I wonder why you haven't," Roger said. "This is an island and I don't believe a ship calls here tonight."

"I do not depend on any ship. Give me the belt."

"We haven't got it," Roger repeated. "Look for yourself, if you aren't convinced."

The man began to move swiftly about the room. He was very quiet. His footsteps were almost soundless on the tiled floor. Only his breathing grew noisier as he slid drawers in and out, raked his hands through folded clothes, opened empty suitcases, searched pockets and found nothing.

When he had pulled all the bedding onto the floor, he suddenly came up close behind Roger.

"You know where it is, you have it somewhere," he said.

"Listen," Roger said, "if we had it or knew where it was, would we have wasted time taking the wrong one to pieces?"

The argument did not penetrate the other man's mind.

"Has the girl got it—your niece?"

"No," Roger said.

Perhaps he said it too quickly or made some involuntary movement.

"I see, she has it," the Frenchman said.

"The murderer has it," said Roger.

"Is she the murderer? She was there in the room." He started to back away from them. "Don't move," he said.

"Don't cry out. Where is the key of this room?" It was lying on the dressing table, so there was no need to answer him. The key and its metal tag clinked together as he picked it up. "I shall now lock this door," he said. "If you make no noise, no one will be hurt."

"You're complicating your own problems a great deal by not using your head," Roger told him.

The man opened the door soundlessly, slipped out and closed it again. There was a soft click as the key was turned on the outside.

Antonia turned away from the wall, listening intently for sounds, any sounds, from the passage. At the same time she wanted to cling tightly to Roger and be told that the ordeal was over, but he had gone straight out onto the balcony, and seeing at once what he intended to do, she found it so hard not to scream that only pressing her hands against her mouth and thinking hard of the man with the gun kept her silent.

The balconies outside the bedrooms were really all one long balcony, separated only by wooden partitions. Roger perched himself on the iron railing that ran along the front of them, grasped the wooden partition and slid one leg around it. Then somehow he wriggled his body after it and, when it had disappeared, drew the other leg out of sight. For a man of his age he was reasonably agile, only suffering from an occasional attack of sciatica in his right leg in cold weather.

Antonia put her ear to the partition, listening for what happened next. She expected startled voices from the room next door, perhaps an outcry. But she heard nothing. Then she realized that the shutters, the tops of which she could see over the partition, were closed, so probably Roger had wasted no time trying to rouse the people inside, but had gone straight onto the next balcony. She leaned out over the railing and saw him in the act of writhing around the farther partition.

He had just vanished when she heard the shot.

The sound seemed to come from the passage, but it echoed so strangely that it might have come from almost anywhere.

After the shot there was a scream, then a door slammed, then there was a blank silence. Then other doors slammed, voices cried out and the passage filled with the sound of running feet.

Antonia ran to the door of her room and started pounding on it.

"Let me out!" she shouted. "Let me out!"

Someone turned the key and opened the door. She plunged out and found herself face to face with Mr. McDougal, who looked at her owlishly out of eyes still reddened by tears.

"Madam, you must forgive me, I know we've met before," he said, "but I can't just recall the time and place. I apologize for such rudeness. I've been under a strain recently, a considerable strain. I hope you'll forgive me. . . ."

She pushed past him. There were other people blocking the passage. She used her elbows fiercely, reached the open doorway of Tessa's bedroom, tried to go in, but found a man standing just inside, his arms spread out to prevent anyone entering.

It was Mr. Ball. When she spoke to him, he began to tell her to keep out, then realized who she was and let her past.

Roger was in the room already, kneeling beside Alec, who was face downward on the floor. He was trying to get up and Roger was trying to stop him. Tessa was standing in the middle of the room, her face dead white and her eyes blank. Antonia went to her and put an arm around her. Tessa was stiff all over. She was not looking at Alec but at the belt of golden coins that lay on the floor at her feet. Antonia was sure that she was not seeing it. If Tessa could see anything at all, it was something in her own head, not in the room.

Then Alec's struggling body suddenly went limp and Tessa at that moment became herself again. She took two swift steps forward and crouched at his side.

"Can you help me?" Roger asked her. "I think we ought to turn him over."

They were starting to move Alec between them when Stanley Smith pushed past Mr. Ball in the doorway, thrust Tessa aside and took her place.

Helping Roger to turn Alec over, Smith said, "I lost him. You can't do much good, following a man with a gun in the dark."

He started to open Alec's shirt. The wound was on his right shoulder and was beginning to bleed freely. Stanley Smith asked Tessa for something to wad over it. She brought a handful of clean handkerchiefs. Then he asked for a pillow from one of the beds. She brought it and he slid it under Alec's head.

"No need to look like that," he said, smiling up at her. "You haven't lost him this time. And the doctor's on the way."

"Is he going to be all right?" Her voice was almost inaudible.

Alec opened his eyes and muttered vaguely, "Tessa, are you . . . ?"

Stanley Smith stood up and moved out of the way. Tessa knelt down beside Alec and slipped a hand into his. He was trying to sit up again.

"Lie still," she said.

Roger had stood up. He went to Antonia's side.

"'A man with a gun can go where he likes until he meets another man with a gun,'" he quoted. "One might add, 'Unless he meets a madman like Alec.'"

"What happened?" she asked.

"I didn't see it. We'll have to ask Tessa. I took too long getting out. The room next door to ours was empty and the shutters were fastened, so I climbed onto the next balcony, and luckily that was Smith's, and just as I was starting to explain why I'd come in that way, we heard the shot. We ran out and saw the Frenchman vanishing through that door that says Emergency Exit. Smith went after him and I came in here. Alec was on the floor and Tessa was standing there like a statue, as if she'd done it herself."

Antonia inconspicuously touched the golden belt on the floor with the toe of her shoe. "He left this behind."

"It wasn't what he wanted."

"But he asked for the other belt."

"I know. I think I know the answer." He spoke closer to her ear. "Don't talk about it to anybody. Literally, to anybody."

The doctor came soon after. He was a short, delicate-looking man with a large, square head set on a neck that looked almost too fragile to support it. He had a fuzz of gray hair standing up from a high lined forehead and anxious eyes behind steel-framed spectacles. His walk was a hurried, scuttling run, as if all his patients were always in danger and he had not much hope of being in time to save them.

He spoke some English, but was glad to have Stanley Smith there to refer to while he repeated at least three times almost everything that he said, going over each statement again and again to make sure that he had been understood. He must operate as quickly as possible, he said, but mercifully the bullet had missed the lung. He would arrange at once for a stretcher and have the young man conveyed to the hospital, where he would have the best of care. Yes, his wife might certainly accompany him, if she wished, unless, that was to say . . . His English broke down in embarrassment, and he murmured something in Greek.

Stanley Smith translated, "Unless the police want Mrs. Foley here. But I expect we can fix that with Mr. Apodiacos. I don't see why they shouldn't talk to her up at the hospital, if that's how she'd like it."

He was looking brisk and confident. There was no sign about him of the nervous strain that Antonia had noticed earlier, but rather the alertness that comes from a pleasing sort of excitement.

Antonia thought sourly, "He's enjoying himself. He likes this. He's feeling fine and important."

However, she admitted that it was useful to have him there when Mr. Apodiacos appeared, as he did a little while later, agreeing quite readily, when Stanley Smith put it to him, that there was no need for Tessa to wait there for the police and she could go with her husband to the hospital.

While they waited for the stretcher party, he asked her to describe what had happened. She answered composedly, still crouching on the floor at Alec's side. There had been a tap at the door, and assuming that it was her aunt or uncle, she had opened it without hesitation. She had found the Frenchman there, pointing a gun at her. He had forced his way in, closed the door and demanded "the belt." She had picked up the belt of gold coins from the dressing table and had handed it to him. He had thrown it down furiously on the floor, grabbed her arm and begun to twist it.

"And that was when Alec rushed at him and the man shot him and ran out and I . . ." Her voice began to shake. "I can't really remember the next bit."

Alec had recovered enough by now to start thanking everyone with his usual grave formality. He even tried it in Greek, replying, *"Efkaristo,"* to everything that was said to him, as if he were competing with the doctor as to which of them could repeat himself most often. The men with the stretcher arrived, lifted him onto it and carried him out. Tessa and Antonia followed.

"I'll join you as soon as I can," Roger told them, "but I've got to talk to Apodiacos first."

As they walked along the rough road, then began to climb the steps up the hill, Antonia wondered if she would ever get to the top. Her feet had been aching before she began the climb and the ache gradually grew into a burning pain that shot up through the soles of her feet into her ankles and started little twinges of cramp in her calves. She soon began to lag behind the others. Tessa, walking along beside the stretcher, did not notice this at first, but when she did she fell back and put an arm through Antonia's.

"Go on," Antonia said. "Stay with him."

Tessa left her arm where it was. "Yes, I suppose I'm going to," she answered, as if she had mistaken Antonia's meaning.

They walked on together, pausing now and then for Antonia to get her breath. The lower steps were mostly in darkness, but the higher they climbed the more lights there were and the more people, who came to see what had happened, wanting to cluster around, commiserate and give advice, but were driven off by swift little forays and shrill exclamations from the doctor.

He kept darting impatiently ahead, then returning to walk beside his patient. The crowd, solemn-faced and sympathetic, formed a little way behind Tessa and Antonia, following up the hill at a slight distance, as Antonia had seen them follow the fishmonger and his donkey. This gave a processional air to their arrival at the hospital, all the more as it was accompanied by conflicting strains from transistors and jukeboxes. At first it astonished Antonia that there were so many people about, then she realized that it was not yet midnight.

The hospital was a small, square building in the heart of the town. It was white, like all the other buildings, with wrought-iron grilles at the windows and a bougainvillaea, making a great splash of purple, lurid in the lamplight, over one wall. The men carried the stretcher in by a side door and Tessa and Antonia followed them.

A nurse appeared and took the two of them to a waiting room. Before they left Alec, they both spoke to him and Tessa bent and kissed him quickly on the lips. On an impulse, before Antonia had had time to think what she was doing, she kissed him too. It was only the second time that she had kissed him. The other time had been when Tessa had just told her that she was going to marry him and before Antonia had learned that he was someone with whom one should not take such liberties. He smiled up at her now and she thought with surprise that Roger had been right, the boy was really quite fond of her.

She did not know how long she and Tessa sat in the waiting room. It was a small, dim room, painted gray, with a gray composition floor and one window, high in the wall. With the smell of antiseptic in the air and the iron grille outside the window, she found herself thinking ungratefully of prison. But hospitals always made her think of prisons, however brightly modern they were. There were straight-backed wooden chairs around the walls and a very large desk, above which hung a large picture. Antonia had sat down on one of the hard chairs and had been gazing vacantly at this picture for some minutes before she took in what it was. It was a very shiny, brightly colored print, in an ornate gold frame, and was of a girl in bed. She was propped up on frilly pillows and covered with a plump pink eiderdown and she was obviously dying of tuberculosis. And on the edge of the bed sat Jesus, neatly bearded, shinily pink of face, wearing a plum-colored robe and with a golden halo, feeling her pulse.

Tessa also was looking at the picture. With a quaver in her voice, she said, "I suppose they have antibiotics too."

"Of course they have," Antonia said, adding firmly, and with more conviction than she felt, "I thought that doctor seemed a most competent man."

"Yes," Tessa said so eagerly that it was plain that she too had her doubts, "I'm sure he is."

Another minute went by very slowly.

"The truth is," Tessa went on, "this is all my fault, isn't it?"

"That's never a very helpful thing to say," Antonia replied, "although of course it generally makes one feel better at the time. I'm feeling awfully tempted to say it's all *my* fault, because—well, because of several things, but I simply won't give in to the impulse."

"What I mean is, if I hadn't bullied you into coming abroad by plane when you didn't want to," Tessa said, "none of this would have happened."

"Something else would probably have happened, which might have been just as bad."

"At least Alec wouldn't have been dragged into it. Only he wasn't exactly *dragged* into it—tonight, I mean. He charged into it like a mad bull. Which was absurd, because I don't think that Frenchman ever meant to shoot anyone. Alec's always so absurd. He overdoes everything. He takes everything so seriously. That's what I couldn't stand about him."

"Well, doing Marriage Guidance, I've listened to a good many complaints about husbands," Antonia said, "but I can't remember that one coming up before."

"Take the bomb, for instance." Tessa was going on talking to try to force the time to pass. "D'you know, he thinks no one's justified in bringing children into the world because he thinks they're sure to be slaughtered by the bomb? So he kept trying to make me go back to the stage, because he said I'd be happier than I was just sitting around, making a mess of the housekeeping."

"Which might be true, as far as it goes. But you want children, do you?"

"Of course I do."

"Didn't you try reminding him that bringing children into the world with plague and smallpox and cholera, and no way of coping with any of them but—" She glanced up at the picture again. "Well, it was quite a hazard too. Yet a good many parents and children seem to have found it relatively worthwhile."

"Yes, of course I did."

"And he gave in, didn't he? He told me he'd agreed to do anything you liked."

"He agreed to do any *damned* thing I liked, which is a bit different."

Antonia gave a sigh. "Yes, I see that. So you left him."

183

"Well, I didn't see how we'd ever sort things out if that was how he felt."

"But you didn't really believe that he meant what he said about the bomb, did you?"

Tessa hesitated. "I did at first. Then I began to realize it went much deeper. It's all tied up with the way he hates his own family, and didn't enjoy his own childhood, and a sort of jealousy of having to share me with his own children." She gave a rueful smile. "Textbook stuff. But knowing that didn't make it any easier. I felt I simply couldn't cope with it all. It was too complicated for me. It rather frightened me, in a way."

"And now?"

Tessa stood up and began to roam about the room.

"I think I've just got to cope with it," she said, "because I've found out I can't live without him." She stood still, looking up at the picture. "That thing's beginning to terrify me. Have we got to hope for a miracle?"

"I rather think the miracle's happened already," Antonia said. "I mean, that Alec wasn't killed on the spot, or even badly hurt."

"You really think he wasn't badly hurt?"

"I'm sure he wasn't."

Tessa sat down again.

"Why don't the police come?"

"There aren't very many of them and I suppose they're out chasing that Frenchman."

Roger arrived a few minutes later, but it was some time before the doctor reappeared. He was wearing a long white coat which had been made for someone a good deal larger than he and had split at the seams. He told them that all was well with Alec, that he had been given a sedative and was sleeping and that there was no point in their waiting any longer. They might return in the morning. Coming to the end of this, he would have repeated it all over again, but they interrupted him with thanks and left.

The way down the hill seemed even longer to Antonia than the way up. But at least the road was almost empty now. Only an occasional figure went quietly by in the darkness, with a soft greeting. Most of the lights in the white boxlike houses had been put out. Sometimes a stamping sound of hooves in a barn, or a sleepy clucking of chickens joined the sound of their own footsteps as they went down the stone stairway. At last the transistors were silent.

They had almost reached the hotel when a tall man suddenly stepped forward out of a patch of dense shadow and stood in front of them. It was Mr. Mobey.

"Mrs. Winfield, isn't this yours?" he said.

He held up in front of her something that gleamed faintly in the starlight. It was a gilded leather belt that had not been slit, with a heavy buckle, set with colored stones, that had not been broken.

# CHAPTER FIFTEEN

"The other belt," Roger said calmly. "May I look at it?"

Mr. Mobey turned to him with a smile. His long pink cheeks were pallid in the darkness, but the gleam of his eyes could be seen.

"You're Professor Winfield," he said. "My name is Mobey. Sam Mobey. May I say it's a remarkable pleasure to meet you, even in the present circumstances, which are not all that one might wish. I'm very well acquainted with your work."

"Thank you," Roger said. "I know of your work too, of course."

"You do, you really do?" Mr. Mobey's teeth flashed as he smiled. "How kind of you at least to say so. I make no pretensions. I'm the veriest amateur."

"A most dedicated amateur, however, a breed disappearing much too fast from this earth."

"Thank you. Thank you indeed. I generally feel we're regarded as a ridiculous anachronism, with too much money to be taken seriously, but not enough, naturally, to emulate the late Mr. Rockefeller in endowing those better trained than ourselves."

"Not at all," Roger said.

Antonia had begun to feel that these courtesies might go on forever. She interrupted. "May I look at the belt, Mr. Mobey?"

He hesitated. "I was on my way to the police with it," he said. "It seemed to me that was the proper course to take. Don't you agree?"

"Oh, entirely," Roger said. "But we've a theory about the thing that we'd like to verify, if you'd just let us take a look at it."

"Ah!" The idea of being present while a theory was being verified seemed to appeal to Mr. Mobey. "It does, of course, belong to your wife, and as for fingerprints, it's been in the sea, so I imagine there's nothing much to be learned." He held the belt out.

"If it's been in the sea, I imagine other things besides fingerprints have been removed," Roger said as he took it. "But still it would be interesting to know if I guessed right about it."

"If you mean, does the thing open up," Mr. Mobey said with a little laugh, "yes, yes, you're quite right. There's a minute screw—hard to see in the dark—let me just show you." He took the buckle out of Roger's hands, pressed a fingernail against the back of the buckle and twisted it. Suddenly the buckle was in two hollow pieces. "There you are, ingenious and quite beautifully made."

"But empty," Roger said.

"Oh yes, quite empty."

"May I ask what made you think of taking it apart?"

"I take no credit for the inspiration at all," Mr. Mobey replied. "Someone had already taken it apart when I found it. The pieces were separate."

"And you found it in the sea?"

"Yes, I was taking my evening swim—I always like to swim early and late, when there's no one else about—and the thing seemed to curl itself about my ankles. I thought for a moment it was some reptile and I felt extremely excited. But that was just wish-fulfillment. There are no creatures along this stretch of coast, at least so close in, with which I had any reason to confuse it. My next thought was seaweed, but as I extricated my leg, I caught the gleam of gold. . . . Oh dear, the thoughts that go through one's head at such a moment! Do any of us ever really grow up, I wonder."

"Very lucky indeed it happened," Roger said, returning the belt to Mr. Mobey. "We'll say goodnight now. I hope very much we'll meet again shortly."

"Tomorrow," Mr. Mobey suggested eagerly. "If you find yourself free at any time tomorrow, or the day after, or any time at all, do please just look in. It would be a great privilege to show you my collection. I'm nearly always at home and always glad of a visit."

With more assurances of mutual esteem, they parted, Mr. Mobey striding off silently and swiftly up the dark road, Roger, Antonia and Tessa going into the hotel.

"My God," Roger exclaimed as soon as he and Antonia had reached their bedroom, "another ten minutes of that man and I'd have been talking just like him."

"You sometimes do anyway," Antonia said. With a groan of relief she kicked off her shoes and collapsed on the bed. "What did you make of his story of finding the belt? Did you believe him?"

"I don't think I believe anyone on this whole blasted island," Roger replied, "unless it's those nice women who gave us coffee this afternoon, and I didn't understand a word they said, so what's the odds?"

"There's always Stanley Smith," Antonia said. "You seem to believe him."

Roger laughed, digging pajamas out of his suitcase.

"Only as far as I can see him, as a matter of fact," he said, "if as far as that. But you might consider this. We know now how the smuggling was normally done. You used to set off from London with the belt you'd got from Madame Julie in your suitcase. You left the case in your sleeper and went along to the dining car and someone, I think that Frenchman, popped in and substituted a normal belt for the one you'd brought with you. That was the trick, the substitution of a belt of the same model as the one you'd brought, so that you'd suspect nothing and there wouldn't be any risk, sometime later on, that you'd stumble on the trick of the buckle yourself and begin to wonder about it. The substitution could be done a lot faster too than unscrewing the buckle and emptying it and screwing it up again. The man would have heard from Julie, of course, what belt you'd bought. . . . But do you remember saying this afternoon that you'd put on weight?"

"Yes," Antonia said.

"You were trying on the belt that had been left in Tessa's room. It was a bit tight, wasn't it? So although it was the same model, the measurements weren't identical. There'd been a slight slip-up there. And I'll tell you another small mistake they made. I saw that it hadn't been worn. Yet you'd worn the belt you'd brought over, hadn't you? You must have, to decide you didn't like it."

"Yes, I wore it the day we came here from Athens," she said.

"And Smith saw you wearing it, didn't he?"

"I suppose so—yes."

"So when the other belt was stolen and returned, he'd have understood what had happened, wouldn't he? That the woman had taken the wrong belt and that you'd still got the one he wanted. Yet he didn't steal it then and there, which he easily could have done if he'd been crooked and had really been after the diamonds all the time. And he wouldn't have had to commit murder to get it."

"Diamonds?" Antonia said. "Who told you it was diamonds?"

"Industrial diamonds," he replied. "I sort of guessed it, as a matter of fact, and I stayed behind when you went to the hospital to see if Apodiacos would confirm it, which he more or less did. London's the center of the diamond trade, you see, and a lot of smuggling goes on. I happened to read about it not long ago. Some Hatton Garden firm found out that thefts from them of small quantities of industrial diamonds had been going on for years. It was thought they were being smuggled out of the country. But to go back to Smith, he only followed instructions and waited to see what was going to happen next, who else would try to get hold of the belt or make contact with you."

"I didn't say anything about his having tried to steal it," Antonia said. "I don't suppose he did."

"But isn't it what you've wondered about ever since you saw him come in covered with all that mulberry juice, which could so easily have covered up bloodstains?"

With a jerk she sat straight up on the bed. "Roger, I've never said a word about that!"

Roger had undressed and had just stretched himself out straight on the other bed with his hands folded under his head.

"But it's what's gone through your mind every time you looked at him," he said.

"Well, suppose it has."

"You see, there needn't have been any bloodstains," he explained. "She was unconscious. He could stick the knife in where he chose and protect himself from the bleeding. And, in fact, since he left the knife in the wound, there wasn't much."

"All right, I won't argue the point," she said. "I'm too tired anyway."

"Tell me something," he said, "did Mobey see you wearing that belt on the journey here? He seemed quite sure it was yours when he found it."

"Yes, but so did lots of other people," she said. "Mr. and Mrs. Ball, Mr. Apodiacos, Dave Lambrick, Mr. McDougal, those Germans and everyone else who came over on the same ship. What's that got to do with it?"

Roger did not answer.

She repeated, "What's that got to do with it, Roger?"

He still did not answer. His eyes had closed, his mouth had fallen open. He was sound asleep.

Antonia got up and began to undress. She was so tired that she kept forgetting what she was doing. Every movement took her twice as long as usual to make, every thought she had became muddled with some other and changed into something quite different from either.

She was conscious of relief that what she had smuggled out of England so often and so successfully had only been diamonds. Stolen, and meaning a financial loss at least to some insurance company, but probably no one in all the world, however scrupulous, has ever broken his heart over the losses of an insurance company. Whereas if it had been heroin or some such thing in the belt, her own heart, for all its innocence, would have been in a pretty bad way at the moment.

Even so, she doubted if she would be able to sleep now. She was too worn out with shock and excitement. What she needed was the peace and quiet of her own home, with nothing to cope with but the housekeeping, and a few friends to see now and then, and a few committees, a few people who couldn't manage their own lives coming to her for her advice. . . .

She stumbled into bed and, with a last hazy question in her mind as to why anyone should come for advice to her, of all people, she fell asleep in a minute.

She was wakened by the maid with the breakfast tray. Her knocking had not wakened Roger. He lay in almost the same position as when he had fallen asleep, peacefully snoring. Antonia went to the door and took in the tray, mixed the instant coffee in the lukewarm water that always arrived for breakfast, then prodded Roger awake.

As he sat up yawning, she said, "Roger, I believe you think Mr. Mobey murdered that girl and stole the diamonds."

"Mobey?" he said. "Who's he?"

But this was merely a phase of his waking up.

"Mobey," he said after he had drunk some coffee. "Awful old humbug. Calls himself an amateur, waiting with his tongue hanging out to be contradicted."

"You were full of compliments to him last night," Antonia reminded him.

"No point in being unpleasant."

"Well, do you think he's the murderer? Did he steal the diamonds?"

Roger bit into a roll. "It's a nice theory. Suppose we go along and see. He asked us to, didn't he?"

"I think he just asked us to visit him and his aquarium, not to investigate him."

"Let's go and visit him and his aquarium, then. See his fishes. I should think, with a hobby like that, some stolen diamonds might come in quite handy, particularly if you aren't really as rich as people think you are."

"Why do you think he isn't as rich as people think he is?"

"Nobody ever is." Roger gulped down the lukewarm brew in his cup. "Listen, I'll try to tell you what's on my mind. I may be all wrong from beginning to end, but here it is. Mobey saw you on the ship coming here when you were wearing the belt you got from that shop."

"Yes, but so did a lot of other people, as I told you just before you fell asleep," Antonia reminded him.

"But they weren't there when the belt was stolen from you in the aquarium."

"Nor was Mr. Mobey. And how could he have known there was anything peculiar about the belt I was wearing on the journey unless he's involved in the diamond smuggling himself? And wouldn't it be altogether too much of a coincidence if he were? I mean, that on the one occasion when all the normal smuggling arrangements went wrong because of the railway strike, I should happen to be coming to the island where he's had a hideout for years."

"If you'd just let me finish . . ."

"All right," she said, "go on."

"He was quite near the aquarium when the other belt was stolen from you," Roger said. "He denied seeing the woman go in or come out, but suppose that wasn't true. Suppose that in fact he saw a peasant woman in black go in and a smart young girl in swimming things come out. He'd find that pretty interesting. Then you arrived and told him what had happened and he happened to know the belt you'd been wearing that day wasn't worth anything. He says nothing about seeing the girl and he does a certain amount of thinking, and later on he sees the same girl walking around with McDougal and he becomes so interested that he begins to keep an eye on her."

"The only thing is," Antonia interrupted, "that he'd have to have amazing eyesight to be able to recognize her, fully dressed, from the mere glimpse he'd have had as she slipped out of the windmill in a swimsuit and cap and went into the sea."

"Not if he had binoculars."

"Well, perhaps it's just possible. So he keeps an eye on her. What next?"

"He sees her go into the hotel, perhaps by that emergency back way that that Frenchman escaped by yesterday. He follows her, sees her go into Tessa's room—"

"How did he know it was Tessa's room?"

"Perhaps he didn't. But he did know it wasn't the girl's room, because he knew by then where she was staying in the town."

"So he follows her in."

"And she turns on him and attacks him and he knocks her out. And then he sees the two belts and begins to understand what had been happening. So he takes the one that had obviously been worn already—"

"And on the bare chance that there's something immensely valuable inside it, murders the girl to prevent her talking and jumps out of the window."

'I wasn't going to say that. I was going to say, he departs as he came and someone else goes in, finds the girl and kills her."

"Why did he produce the belt last night, then? Why didn't he simply throw it away for someone else to find, or really hide it, so that it would never be found? He might have fed it to his fishes, for instance. I'm sure some of those monsters would gobble up anything."

"Feed it to his . . . ?" Roger stared at her. His eyes

were suddenly very bright. "Not the belt, no, but the diamonds! Where could you find a better hiding place for them than among all the sand and weed in a fish tank? You could leave them there indefinitely and sift them out at your leisure when all the fuss and bother had died down. Come on, let's go and visit Mr. Mobey and his fish."

He tore off his pajamas in great haste, darted into the bathroom and turned on the shower.

Antonia was not in a mood to dress so hastily. She took her time and when she was ready, found, as she had expected, that a good deal of Roger's enthusiasm had died. They went first to Tessa's room, but she had already gone out. As they went downstairs together in a rather somber silence, Roger had a puzzled frown on his face, as if he were wondering why he had been so sure of his argument only a little while before.

Mrs. Marinatos met them at the bottom of the stairs.

"I have a message for you from Mrs. Foley," she said. "She has gone to the hospital to see her husband. He is better, I am happy to say. I have telephoned the doctor to ask. Monsieur Marais, the man who shot him, has regrettably not been found. Also I have to tell you the police have arrested the murderer. It is Mr. McDougal. I am very glad it is not any guest in this hotel. It is very bad to have it happen here, but good that he and the girl are not guests here."

Her brisk tone suggested that since the people had not been guests, everything could now return to normal.

Roger and Antonia walked out into the sunlight. They took the path that led behind the cottages toward the windmill. The glare was no fiercer than usual, the heat was no more oppressive, but almost at once Antonia's head began to ache. The flower scents in the air only seemed nauseating. When a donkey went past with two young boys on its back, their laughing greeting, "Goodbye-ice-cream!" and their charming, impish smiles failed to amuse her.

Roger was still frowning and his face looked drawn, as if he too were suffering from some malaise, perhaps the first symptoms of food poisoning. When they had gone a little way he said, "McDougal—no."

"Yet he's made to measure for your theory that the belt was stolen by Mr. Mobey and the murder done by somebody else."

"Yes, but he was fairly drunk last night, and when he's drunk he confides in women and apologizes to them, he doesn't murder them."

"Yes, and he gives them flowers. But I don't believe that argument would stand up in a court of law."

They walked on. The traffic on the path was busy that morning, far busier than in the afternoon when Antonia had been followed along it by the woman in black. They had to flatten themselves against the hedge again and again to let strings of mules and donkeys go by with their broad, swaying loads.

At a bend in the path they suddenly came face to face with a figure in black and Antonia felt her heart absurdly pounding. But the figure was a priest, a tall, muscular figure with a gray beard of great magnificence and large boots showing under his habit and a little bunch of herbs in his hand that no doubt he was taking home to his cook.

Mr. Mobey was on his veranda. He was reclining in a long chair, reading a solid-looking volume that was supported on his stomach, but when he saw Roger and Antonia he sprang very nimbly to his feet and came to meet them with hand outstretched.

"The very thing that I was hoping for," he said. "It's been on my mind all the morning that you might come, particularly as it seems that unfortunate affair at your hotel has been wound up and I don't suppose the police are bothering you any more. *Crime passionelle* after all. It usually is, I suppose. Just your great misfortune that it should have happened in your niece's room. The mysterious business about the two belts probably had nothing to do with it. The poor girl bolted into the room, no doubt, trying to escape from the fellow, then turned on him with her knife in an effort to save herself, was knocked out and cold-bloodedly stabbed. Nasty, very nasty. The moral is, always lock your door, even on an island where no one ever locks up anything. But let's forget about it. Is it too early to offer you a drink?"

Replying that he rather thought it was, Roger said, "You seem to have heard all about it."

"The island grapevine," Mr. Mobey replied. "The most efficient system of communication in the world, always allowing for an element of distortion. Some of my facts may be not quite as perfectly accurate as one could wish. Being more on the spot, you may be able to put me right here and there. Well, if the idea of a drink doesn't appeal to you yet, can I persuade you to come over to the aquarium with me? Mrs. Winfield, would you face its dangers again, accompanied this time by two strong men?"

It was a moment that Antonia had been dreading. The thought of going down again into that dank, submarine stench and finding her way along that rock passage where she would be expecting every shadow to yield up an evil presence had been weighing on her mind all the way from the hotel. Probably it was almost as much responsible for her sick headache as her dismay at the arrest of poor Mr. McDougal. But she had made up her mind that if Roger wanted to go down into the place, she was going with him. So she smiled and said that nothing could be more interesting than being conducted around the aquarium by Mr. Mobey himself.

As they walked across the stretch of sand between the house and the windmill, they were hailed by a stout figure in swimming trunks, a broad-brimmed hat and sunglasses. Mr. Apodiacos was out again, hunting for shells and pretty pebbles for his daughters. But the man who had let Antonia into the mill before, taken her three drachmas from her and later come to her rescue was nowhere to be seen. He took charge, Mr. Mobey explained, only in the afternoons. He himself attended to the tanks and looked after the place in the mornings.

His talk, which flowed on as they strolled around among the glass cases on the ground level, then went down the white-tiled staircase, lessened for Antonia the claustrophobia that assaulted her when they reached the bottom and stepped through the stone archway into the dim passage beyond. It was becoming increasingly fascinating talk, for in spite of his mannerisms, his mock modesty and his coy jokes, he was a passionate enthusiast. At each tank he stopped and spoke lovingly, illuminatingly about the creatures inside, making a kind of music of their unbeautiful Latin names, and with fluid gestures of his large, soft hands drawing attention to grace, color and strangeness in form and movement.

They moved on very slowly. Roger said very little, yet he stood a long time at each tank, his face intent and a curious light in his eye. Because Antonia was feeling the spell of the place even more strongly than she had before, she wondered if it were possible that Roger's concentration, his peering through bubbles and weed and greenish water, was all in a hunt for a handful of industrial diamonds, or if he had simply forgotten all about them and lost himself in the underwater world, as she had herself when the woman in black had pounced on her.

At last, working their way along the curving passage, they came to the point where it had happened. There was the big tank where the turtles swam on and on in their stately figures of eight and there beyond it was the patch of shadow in which something had moved, although Antonia had been too absorbed to notice.

Nothing moved there now. But as before, the shadow had more substance than a shadow should. It had a head, arms, legs and the face—what was left of it—of the missing Frenchman. A gun lay on the damp stone floor at his side.

# CHAPTER SIXTEEN

"Ouzo," Mr. Apodiacos said. "You must drink ouzo. Nothing opens the appetite and makes gay so quickly."

He had so completely taken charge that nobody argued with him. Nobody said that this was not a time for being gay. They accepted the word as having only a relative meaning. He went into Mr. Mobey's house and in a minute or two returned with a tray, a bottle, water and glasses to the veranda where Mr. Mobey had collapsed in a long chair. His eyes were tight shut and his well-fleshed body was limp and twitching.

Mr. Apodiacos poured out the ouzo, added water and handed the glasses around. Then he went indoors again. The telephone tinkled. Antonia sipped the milky fluid, which she had never liked and which made her think of the cough mixtures of her youth, but at least it had a medicinal effect on her now. The blurred outlines of Roger and Mr. Mobey became sharp, the sea became still and quiet, instead of rolling as if she were on a Channel steamer in a gale.

But how wonderful it would be to be on a Channel steamer, even in a gale, so long as it was homeward bound!

She took another sip and realized that Roger was talking quietly to Mr. Mobey.

"You said people don't lock up anything on this island. Does that mean you don't lock that place up at night?"

"Why should I, will you tell me that?" Mr. Mobey demanded querulously, as if Roger had been accusing him of a grave failure of normal caution. "Who's going to walk away with a lot of fish? Who's going to think of spending the night in a damp, noisome place like that? Who's going to think of using it for immoral purposes? Who's going to care if they do? Who in his senses is going to go in there and commit suicide? And what else is there to worry about?"

"So there's no problem about how the man got in there," Roger said. "It could have happened any time during the night."

"Certainly," Mr. Mobey said.

"And is it generally known that you don't lock up at night?"

"Undoubtedly. Everything is known on this island. A more absurd place for committing a murder couldn't have been found. If it was a murder, which I can see in your eye is what you believe. Personally I think it was suicide."

"If it was murder, they seem to have arrested the wrong man," Roger said. "Assuming that the girl and this man were killed by the same person."

Mr. Apodiacos, coming out on to the veranda again and sipping from his glass, said, "I hear what you say, Professor Winfield, and you are quite right. Mr. McDougal did not leave the hotel yesterday evening until he was arrested. He had no chance to come here, meet Mr. Marais and kill him. But already last night I know he is not the murderer."

"Then why arrest the poor devil?" Roger asked.

Mr. Apodiacos shrugged his naked shoulders up to his ears. "A mistake; but I tell you something," he said, "I am very happy to be under arrest when there is a murderer loose. I am safe. I do not have to go out and help catch a murderer and perhaps be shot at myself. I wish someone would arrest me now."

It was a nice answer, even if it did not answer Roger's question. Standing looking down at Mr. Mobey, Mr. Apodiacos sipped some more ouzo. It had not yet started to make him very gay.

"Mr. Mobey," he said, "when you took that belt to the police last night and told them how you found it in the sea, was it the truth you told them?"

"Of course it was," Mr. Mobey answered petulantly. But after a moment he went on, "No, it wasn't. Nearly, but not quite. The actual truth places me in a slightly discreditable light. I realize, however, that I'd better make up my mind to face that. The truth is, I didn't find the belt in the sea by chance. I saw someone throw it in."

"You *saw* him? You saw who?" Mr. Apodiacos asked swiftly.

"A shadow," Mr. Mobey replied. "A shadow moving quietly along the beach. And having heard of the murder in the hotel and suffering, as I do, from more imagination than has ever been really useful to me, I was afraid to go up to him and speak to him, or even to follow at a distance. I admit it. For all I knew it might be only yourself or Professor Winfield, but still I was afraid. So I waited until I couldn't hear his footsteps any more, then I went into the sea to look for what he'd thrown in. The sea was so still I found it quite easily. In fact, it had not even sunk yet. It hadn't occurred to him to roll it up and weight it with a stone."

"What time was this?" Mr. Apodiacos asked.

"Perhaps about midnight."

"And which way was he walking, toward the windmill or away from it?"

"Toward it."

"Didn't you hear or see him go in?"

"No. That is—well, he might have. But I told you, I was afraid. Do I have to repeat it?" Mr. Mobey sounded offended at having this required of him. "I preferred not to investigate and in fact I didn't go into the mill till I had the company of Professor and Mrs. Winfield."

"A shadow," Antonia murmured, " 'a little shadow that goes in and out with me . . .' Mr. Apodiacos!"

He turned to her.

She said, "You know who it is, don't you? Why are you shielding him?"

The ouzo might not have opened her appetite yet, but certainly it had opened her understanding and made all sorts of things wonderfully clear.

As Mr. Apodiacos only continued to look at her without speaking, she nodded earnestly.

"You've understood what happened ever since Mr. Mobey took the second belt to the police last night," she said. "You almost said so when you admitted they'd been wrong to arrest Mr. McDougal."

He gave a sardonic smile. "Mrs. Winfield, you are always so sure of so much. I wish I had your wisdom. Will you please tell me whom I should not shield?"

"Stanley Smith."

Sunglasses cannot change their expression. Those of Mr.

Apodiacos only continued to glare blankly. But anger showed in the set of his plump lips. At the same time Antonia heard Roger's faint intake of breath. She thought that he was going to speak, to try to stop her going on, but he only shook his head at her, giving her up as hopeless.

She shook her head back at him. "I know you think I've an obsession about the man, Roger," she said. "And of course I have, and no wonder. But that doesn't mean I'm wrong, does it? That isn't logic."

"No," he agreed, "but I explained . . ." He broke off, leaving the argument to better men than he.

She went on, "You explained that if Stanley Smith was crooked and had been meaning to get the diamonds for himself all the time, he could have got away with my belt at any time and without having to commit a murder. But you see, he couldn't."

"Why not?"

"Because of Mr. Apodiacos."

The Greek gave one of his more sinister, less good-natured smiles. "I am not sure if you compliment my intelligence, or suggest I had already taken the diamonds," he said.

"I meant simply," she answered, "that until yesterday, the day of the murder, you and Stanley Smith were the only people here who knew there were diamonds in the belt. So if I'd complained that I'd had another belt stolen, you'd have known who'd taken it."

"The girl knew," he said, "the girl who took the first one."

"But she didn't know there was another belt. On the journey here, when I was wearing it, she was being so careful that I shouldn't see her that she never got close

enough to me to see it. If she had, she'd never have stolen
the other one." She finished her ouzo. "If you like, I can
tell you how the whole thing happened and I can prove
it too. At least, I can tell you how to prove it."

"Thank you," Mr. Apodiacos said with ironical humility.
"How shall I prove it?"

"You must question your daughters."

"My daughters? These young children?"

"Young children are often very truthful."

"Certainly, certainly. But these, let me tell you, have a
great liking for my friend Smith."

"Smith?" a voice said behind Antonia. "Talking about
me?" And Stanley Smith lounged out from behind the trel-
lis at the end of the veranda.

Mr. Mobey gave a start and looked all around him, as
if he thought that other unexpected people might appear.
Mr. Apodiacos showed no surprise. Antonia thought that
he had probably been watching Stanley Smith approaching along the shore. Roger tried to catch Antonia's eye and
hold it with a look of warning, but she looked away.

"You are here before the police," Mr. Apodiacos said to
the young man as he sat down on the edge of the veranda
and brought cigarettes out of his pocket.

"I hadn't so far to come," Smith said. "Do we go over
and take a look at the body, or do we wait for them?"

"I think we wait."

"All right." Smith smiled up at Antonia. "Go on, Mrs.
Winfield, don't let me interrupt you. Get it out of your system. You'll never be happy till you do. Say any damned
thing you like about me. I won't hold it against you."

"Then you overheard what I was saying," she said.

"Some of it, and I don't blame you," he replied. "You've
had a lot to put up with. I'm just rather sorry about it.

The more I've had to trail around at your heels, the better I've been getting to like you. But it doesn't seem to have worked in reverse."

She shook her head. "No."

"Pity," he said. "Well, go on."

"Please, Mrs. Winfield!" Mr. Apodiacos broke in, flapping his hands up and down. "Let us talk of something else, shall we? Murder is for the police. Let us wait for them."

"I believe you really *are* shielding him," she said with a frown. "Or are you worrying because I said you ought to question your daughters? It's nothing that need upset them. All you have to do is ask them if they spilled a bowl of mulberries over Mr. Smith yesterday evening, or if he did it himself. And I think you'll find he did it himself, because when he followed the girl into my niece's room and she turned on him and attacked him, she scratched him with her knife somewhere on his chest and it bled a certain amount and stained his shirt. And he couldn't just go about without the shirt, because it would have shown the cut, and he knew he couldn't get up to his room to change the shirt without being seen, so he smothered himself in mulberry juice. Of course he hadn't really been along the shore and found the black dress in the dark by chance. He'd found it sometime earlier and hidden it somewhere until he'd decided how to use it. But saying he'd just found it made it sound as if he'd been a fair distance from the hotel when the murder happened."

"I see, I see," Mr. Apodiacos said in a tone of resignation. "Now we know everything, eh?" He was careful not to look at the smiling Stanley Smith.

But Antonia was looking at him intently, critically, as she had been looking at him at every opportunity that had occurred during the last week. Probably he had never in all his life been looked at as carefully as he had by her during that week. Probably no one else, not even a woman in love with him, had ever become as sensitive as Antonia had to the slightest change of expression on his sharp-featured face, or the changes of muscular tension in his angular body. So now she had noticed at once the changes, not in his smile or the look in his eyes, but in the set of his shoulders and the curious clumsiness of his hands as he fiddled with his cigarette.

She went on, "I don't believe he meant to murder the girl or steal the diamonds when he went into the room. With Mr. Apodiacos here, working with him, he wouldn't have thought there was any chance of his getting away with it. But she turned on him and attacked him and he had to knock her out. And then he saw the two identical belts and understood how the smuggling was done. Till then he hadn't been absolutely sure exactly how it was worked. And Mr. Apodiacos still didn't know. So Mr. Smith thought that if he killed the girl and stole the one belt and left the other behind, no one would know. No one but Monsieur Marais, who'd brought the second belt with him and given it to the girl to exchange for the other one, and whom Mr. Smith chased down the stairs after he'd shot Alec Foley and lost so quickly in the darkness. What did you tell him, Mr. Smith? That you'd do a deal with him? That you'd meet him in the mill later?" She looked back at Mr. Apodiacos. "If you don't believe me, why don't you ask him to open his shirt and show you whether or not he's got a cut on his chest?"

Still Mr. Apodiacos did not move, but Roger suddenly did, turning on Stanley Smith and reaching out for the opening of his checked shirt. Smith writhed out of his grasp and ran. Roger lunged after him, but he was twenty years the older and much too slow. Mr. Mobey came excitedly up from his chair, but tripped and nearly fell. Mr.

207

Apodiacos shook his head, clicked his tongue and walked with deliberation in Smith's wake around the corner of the house and stood there looking after him.

Two perspiring policemen were coming tramping along the path at the back of the house. Mr. Apodiacos shouted at them and waved at the fleeing figure that was already halfway across the field opposite and heading for the shelter of an olive grove at the base of a pine-covered hill. They began to run after him, but they were middle-aged men and the distance between them lengthened and in a minute or two Stanley Smith had vanished among the trees.

That was the last that Antonia ever saw of him.

"Mad," Mr. Mobey said. "Mad panic. You frightened him out of his wits, Mrs. Winfield. He can't possibly get away."

"Of course he can't get away," Mr. Apodiacos said with extreme irritation. "But now we shall never, never get the diamonds back. There was only one way to get them back and that was to let him think no one knew he was the murderer and to let him leave and arrest him on the launch from the harbor to the ship, because then he must have had them on him or in his luggage. Now they are lost, gone. Oh, Mrs. Winfield, why must you be so right and so sure all the time? Why had you not just a few doubts? Then perhaps you would have been silent. Only about one thing you are wrong. My daughters. I have no daughters. None. These are my sister's children. It is convenient when I am sent here to watch you to appear to have a reason for coming, so I bring my sister and her children for a holiday. Otherwise, why should I come? What Greek goes anywhere for peace and quiet? Peace and quiet!"

Muttering it under his breath, he left them, strolling

out into the fields to meet the policemen, who had stood still and were consulting what to do next.

They found Stanley Smith two days later, but Mr. Apodiacos had been right, they never found the diamonds. Perhaps Smith had left them in a hole in the sand, or under a stone, or perhaps he had simply scattered them in the dust as he ran, knowing that they would never be of any use to him. Or perhaps, Roger suggested to Antonia, clinging to his theory, but only in private, Mr. Mobey had them all the time. Perhaps the truth about his finding of the belt was that he had seen Smith bury it in the sand after the murder and before hurrying along to the police with it, like a law-abiding member of the island community, had helped himself to the diamonds. In which case, what better hiding place for them than one of his fish tanks?

Whatever the truth of that matter, Stanley Smith was dead when he was found on some rocks at the foot of a cliff by some fishermen whose boats were beached nearby. It was thought that he might have been trying to steal one of the boats to attempt to escape but had slipped on the steep path in the darkness and fallen.

Roger and Antonia heard the news from Mrs. Marinatos. The hotel was almost empty just then. The bus and the two taxis had left for the harbor, taking away most of the guests, and had not yet returned with that day's new arrivals. Among others, Mr. and Mrs. Ball had gone, with McDougal in tow. So had the two Germans, who had left as they had come, conversing endlessly and ignoring everything around them but one another. Dave Lambrick had gone, taking a seat in the bus as far from the Balls as he could and starting to work on a chess problem.

The Winfields had thought of leaving, but had been asked by the police to remain at least until Stanley Smith had been found and until certain matters connected with the smuggling of the diamonds had been cleared up. But the real inquiry concerning them awaited Antonia in England, where, Mr. Apodiacos had told her, Madame Julie and several other people involved in regular thefts of industrial diamonds from a Hatton Garden firm had already been arrested. So, among other troubles, Antonia thought, feeling shocked at her own triviality, she would have to find somewhere else to buy her clothes. . . .

But one or two good things had come out of the holiday, if a holiday was what you could call it.

First, there was the change in Tessa and Alec.

With his arm in a sling and his face pale under the beginnings of a sun tan, Alec was rebellious at having to take things quietly and Tessa had her work cut out trying to make him lie down when he was supposed to and not take longer walks than he ought. It was very good for her. For Alec too. It led to a happy sort of wrangling, which generally ended with Alec saying that he would do any damned thing that Tessa wanted, a remark that had become a private joke of theirs and led to laughter, which would leave off suddenly as they looked with loving seriousness at one another. They were both charming to Roger and Antonia, but did not know that they existed.

The other good thing that had resulted was the fancy that Roger had taken to the island, to its climate, its food, its people and even, apparently, to the aquarium and Mr. Mobey, with whom Roger seemed happy to spend so much time that it was evident he was really convinced of his theory and meant sooner or later to discover where Mr. Mobey had hidden the diamonds.

Anyway, it kept him interested. Sitting on the terrace, waiting for lunch, after a quiet morning of swimming and lying in the sun, he said, as he had said once before, that he thought he and Antonia ought to return next year when things were normal.

"Normal? Are conditions anywhere ever normal?" she demanded. "One always strikes the wettest, or the hottest, or the windiest season that's been heard of in that spot for years. This year, someone's probably going to tell us, we've just been unlucky and struck the most murderous."

"Well then, the probabilities are that it'll be nice and quiet next year," Roger said. "What about it?"

She smiled. Next year was a long way off and there were hundreds of other beautiful islands in this shining sea.